Tangerine
for the
Executioner's
Rope

Tangerine for the Executioner's Rope

A Frank Fitzpatrick Novel

Robert X. Burgess

For Charlotte

…the State is nothing more nor less
than a bandit gang writ large…
—Murray Rothbard, *The Ethics of Liberty*

One

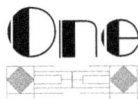

The beach was crowded that August morning. About twenty feet away from me, a group of men and women in their early twenties played volleyball. A woman squealed after slapping the ball. A man on the opposite side of the net leaped, spiked the ball, and drove the ball into the sand, where the ball bounced, left an intaglio, and scored a point for his team. The woman groaned.

A breeze redolent of sea salt and suntan lotion wafted in from the Atlantic. I smiled. Life felt good, and life felt right on that Florida beach.

I was at Louie's, my favorite bistro, in a chaise lounge under a white, blue, and gold umbrella advertising Corona. I was waiting for an old friend, Candy Vogel, who had called me the previous evening from Las Vegas. She had refused to tell me over the phone what was wrong, saying that she needed to speak to me in private and that it was urgent. I had offered to pick her up at the airport, but she had declined, saying that she did not want to inconvenience me. I had given her the address of Louie's, and she had said that she would meet me there at ten.

A woman shrieked. I jerked my head. One of the volleyball players—a darkly tanned woman wearing a red Speedo one-piece—nursed her elbow, while a woman, who appeared to be the wounded player's identical twin, ran over to help. I looked toward the boardwalk and saw Mrs. Means, my neighbor. She was walking Santiago, her black, standard-sized poodle. Mrs. Means nodded. I nodded. Santiago barked.

I spotted Candy Vogel among tourists crowding the boardwalk. I waved. The Atlantic breeze tugged at a scarf covering her platinum-colored hair. Her bright red lips were pursed, and her oval-shaped face was pale, as if coated in pancake. She was wearing sunglasses, so I couldn't see her eyes, but I had a hunch that

1

they looked rheumy. Even though she had never been a professional dancer, she had the legs of a professional dancer, legs that would drive any straight man to lust. She reminded me of Marilyn Monroe, when Monroe was nearing the end of her tragic life.

I motioned for Candy to have a seat in the other chaise lounge under the white, blue, and gold umbrella advertising Corona.

"Crazy eights," I said.

It was our code from way back when, when I had lived in Las Vegas and had worked with her then-new husband, Arthur. He had coined the term after winning over ten thousand dollars on a Crazy Eights slot machine at the Barbary Coast Casino.

"If the circumstances were different, I would say that it was good to see you too, Frank."

"You said that you had something urgent to discuss with me."

"I would have told you over the phone, but I needed to see you."

"What is it, Candy? What's going on? Does Arthur know that you're here?"

"This is about Arthur," she said. "He's been missing since Monday evening."

This was Thursday morning. I exhaled. "Did he make it to the Nevada Test Site on Monday?"

"Yes, he did." She sighed—really, more of a soft choke—and I knew that she was doing her best not to cry. "He left as usual at five-forty-five sharp. And he made it to the Test Site. Maxine told me. He was there all day."

"Did anyone see him leave?"

"No one saw him leave."

"Have you made any formal statements to the police, to the FBI, or to Maxine or her people?"

"No, I haven't, Frank. Why?"

"We'll talk about that later."

Alfredo, my waiter, placed a bottle of chilled Perrier water, along with a chilled glass, in front of me. I ordered chilled Perrier water for Candy. Alfredo said that he would go get the drink.

"They found his car," she said.

"Where?"

"At a Smith's over on Rainbow Boulevard. One of the grocery sackers came to check on the Jag because it had been there all night."

"Any signs of violence? Anything on the store cameras?"

Candy shook her head. "No signs of violence. The windows were up, and the doors were locked. It was like he had gone into the store to get milk and never came back. And the security cameras weren't working, so there's no security tape."

I looked at an Arctic blue horizon. A seagull cried overhead. The volleyball game resumed, and the young people laughed.

"Is it possible that Arthur ran off with another woman?" I said. "I know that you and Arthur had issues in your marriage."

"Arthur and I did have issues in our marriage," she said, sounding as if she were getting angry or bitter, perhaps both. "But we resolved those issues. Arthur forgave me for the affair. And he's not the type to seek revenge by having an affair of his own."

"What have the Las Vegas police discovered?"

"Nothing," she said.

"The FBI?"

"Nothing."

"Maxine's people?"

"Nothing," she said, sounding very bitter.

I rubbed my unshaved chin and poured chilled Perrier water into the chilled glass. The water gurgled pleasantly. Alfredo placed a bottle of chilled Perrier water in front of Candy and set a chilled glass in front of her. I thanked him.

"You're welcome, Mr. Fitzpatrick," Alfredo said, and he hurried off to tend to other patrons.

Candy and I were silent a few moments.

"What does Maxine have to say about all of this?" I said.

"She said that she and her people are working on it and that they're going to find Arthur."

"You don't sound so sure, Candy."

"That's because I'm not."

"And how do you think I can help?"

"You and Arthur are alike. You think logically. You like to reflect before you say anything and before you act. You believe in

3

reason. When we used to hang out on the Strip, it was you who always found Arthur when he wandered off."

"It's obvious that you want me to go back to Las Vegas with you and search for Arthur. Even if I did go, I'm not so sure that I would do any good."

"You have to find him, Frank," she said.

"He and I didn't part on the best of terms, as you know."

"That's why I came down here. You might have said no over the phone. But I know that you won't say no to me in person."

I stared at her.

"You have to find him, Frank."

"And what if I don't find him?"

"You have to, Frank. You owe it to him, remember?"

Arthur, using cucumber-cool words, had prevented Robinson from poniarding the razor-sharp tip of an Italian stiletto into my carotid. So, on that count, I did, indeed, owe Arthur.

"All right," I said. "I'll go with you. But I can't promise that I'll find him."

"Thank you, Frank." Candy removed her sunglasses. As I had suspected, her eyes were rheumy. The pupils in her ice blue irides became pinpoints. "I purchased a ticket for you. Our flight takes off at three, so we don't have much time."

I stood. "I'll be ready with my things in half an hour."

I left money on the table to cover the chilled Perrier waters, left a hefty tip, and Candy and I left the bistro on the crowded beach.

The volleyball game ended in conjunction with our departure.



On the flight to Las Vegas, Candy told me the story. There were several trivial details. The essential details, however, were these: two months earlier, Arthur had become close friends with a non-objective painter, Zsa Zsa Cortez, who had a studio north of old Las Vegas.

There had been the incident at one of Zsa Zsa's parties, to which Arthur and Candy had been invited. Arthur had gotten into a heated argument with Eliot Waxwell, one of Las Vegas's new big-time players and Cortez's patron. Candy had never seen Arthur so angry. After the party, Arthur had refused to discuss the argument.

After we landed, Candy drove us in her Mercedes up the 15, and soon we connected with the 95. We headed north, where we exited on Lake Mead Boulevard. Then we headed west to Summerlin, where Candy and Arthur lived.

"I've heard about Maxwell," I said. "On the rare occasion, I take a look at the *National Enquirer* just to see how much further our country has gone down the toilet. Wasn't he dating some diva?"

"It's Waxwell, not Maxwell," she said. "He thinks he's God's gift to this world, women, and Las Vegas, in that order. When he isn't trying to outdo Steve Wynn, Waxwell's chasing any rich skirt that he sees. They call him the new Richard Branson. It seems that Waxwell not only wants to take over Las Vegas, he wants to expand into the recording and airlines industries and conquer these, too. And the diva you mentioned was Celine Dion, by the way."

"I wouldn't know," I said.

"I know you wouldn't," said Candy, and she looked over and smiled at me. Her face didn't look so pale now; in fact, it looked very healthy. "You're not one for things current, are you?"

"Except for technology, when it's useful. I'm not a Luddite, you know."

"Oh, I know that."

"Arthur seems to have made high friends in high places, in a relatively short amount of time."

"I think Zsa Zsa Cortez considers him a pet," Candy said. "You know how no one can stump Arthur with math puzzles and problems. Zsa Zsa likes it when Arthur entertains at parties. And you know how quickly Arthur can compute cube roots and so forth. It's one of the reasons why I married him."

Candy and I entered Summerlin. About ten minutes later, she drove the Mercedes into a cul-de-sac and into the driveway of a stucco, two-story house.

Inside, I examined Arthur's desk and a few of his handwritten notes. I didn't find anything suspicious. After my search, Candy stepped into the kitchen and checked the landline for messages.

She called one of the FBI agents who had left a message for her and then told me that she was going to call Maxine. I went into the den to catch the evening news. That night's main story was about the explosion of drug smuggling into the Southwest and how the US Border Patrol and how the DEA were having difficulty catching a majority of the shipments.

Ten minutes later, Candy appeared in the living room and poured herself a shot of peppermint schnapps. She asked if I wanted anything. I said a soda water, if she had it, and she said that she did.

The chilled glass felt cold and comforting in my hands. Candy sat on a loveseat, diagonal to my chair, and curled her legs up underneath her. I sipped my soda water. She used a remote control to turn off the television set.

"Any word from Las Vegas PD?" I said.

"Please, don't even mention those clowns," she said. "Larsen, the FBI agent, said that they had leads in Ogden, Utah, and in Farmington, New Mexico. Maxine said pretty much the same thing."

"Those places aren't very close together," I said. "Ogden's to the north of Salt Lake City. Farmington's in the Four Corners area. This means that they don't have anything substantial."

"Do you think he's dead, Frank?" She said this with some hesitation.

"I don't know, Candy. And even if I did know, I'm not sure that I would want to say."

"What do your instincts tell you?"

"I don't believe in instincts," I said, "I believe in reason. If you're asking me what reason says, reason says that we need to keep our heads cool and not do something foolish, like driving around all night in a vain search for Arthur. Reason says that we must think and act calmly at all times. Reason says that I should go first thing in the morning to meet with Zsa Zsa Cortez and to see what she can tell me."

"He," Candy said.

"He?"

"Zsa Zsa is a man, Frank." She paused. "A rather strange, exotic man, as you'll discover. His real name is Enrique, by the way."

I leaned back in my chair and closed my eyes. I was tired, but if I had to, if Candy needed me to, I could stay awake all night.

"Frank?"

"Yes?" I opened my eyes and looked at Candy.

"I'm scared. I'm really scared."

I placed my glass on a coaster on an end table, stood, and went over to the loveseat where Candy was sitting. I sat down beside her and placed an arm around her. I am not a touchy-feely man, but I did my best to comfort her. She placed her head on my shoulder and cried. Then she apologized, excused herself, and rushed out of the living room.

Candy returned to the living room a few moments later, clutching a handful of tissues.

"Whatever you have to do, do it," Candy said. "I want Arthur back. Please promise me that you'll bring him back."

"I promise that I'll do my best, Candy. That's all that I can promise."

She nodded. I handed her the shot of schnapps, which she finished. I returned to my chair and finished my soda water. She turned on the television set, and we watched the remainder of the local news. After the news was over, Candy hugged me, kissed my forehead, and then told me goodnight.

I bade her goodnight and then turned in for the evening.

TWO

Next morning, Candy and I ate a breakfast of bacon, fried eggs, and black coffee, which I had prepared. She sat at the kitchen counter, wearing Christmas candy-striped pajamas, her platinum-colored hair tied back into a ponytail. I stood. We watched the news, which included a brief report about the ongoing search for Arthur, along with a story about the increase of heroin trafficking in the greater Las Vegas area.

Candy snapped off the television set. She handed me a scrap of paper, upon which she had written, in italic, Zsa Zsa Cortez's address and Maxine's contact information.

"Just be wary," she said. "He's a creep who likes to play games with people. I never liked him. And I never saw what Arthur saw in him."

"I intend to find out," I said, placing the scrap of paper into my shirt pocket. I rubbed my chin, which was freshly shaved. Lenny, who was a good friend because I had rescued his wife and his second-grade daughter from a serial rapist, had dropped off a Toyota Prius for me earlier that morning. "You have my cell phone number. Call me if anything comes up. I plan to be out most of the day, if not all of it."

I drove the Prius out of the cul-de-sac. Several cars sped up and down the street. I injected myself into the traffic, which flowed like a rapidly moving creek to Lake Mead Boulevard. From there I took the exit ramp, heading south on the 95.

Zsa Zsa's studio, an old warehouse, took up an entire city block. A ten-foot-high concrete wall surrounded the building. A semicircular porte-cochere acted as the sole entrance. I drove through it and parked the Prius next to a black Harley-Davidson. I stepped out of the car and headed up a concrete ramp leading to a large, wooden door. The August air felt like a furnace blast.

I pushed a button labeled DOORBELL. A moment passed. The intercom next to the button came alive with a hissing sound, like a freshly awakened rattlesnake in the desert.

"Yes?" a voice said, sounding tired, sounding petulant.

"My name's Frank Fitzpatrick. I'm a friend of Arthur and Candy Vogel. I was wondering if I could ask you a few questions about Arthur."

"Who?"

"Arthur. Arthur Vogel."

"No, no, silly, who? Who are you?"

"Frank Fitzpatrick. I'd like to ask you a few questions about Arthur."

"Like what, my dear?"

"Why don't you come and find out?"

"Oh, my, you are something else, aren't you?" the voice said, giggling. "Be down in a jiff."

I heard an elevator hum. The door opened, held in place by a chain. A man barely over five feet tall peered out at me. He was wearing black-framed, thick-lensed glasses. Gel held his thick, black, combed-back hair in place. He was definitely Filipino, among other things.

"Who are you again?" he said.

"Frank Fitzpatrick, Mr. Cortez."

"My, aren't we so formal? For a hunk like you, it's Zsa Zsa. Are you a cop?"

"No, just a friend of Arthur and Candy Vogel, as I said."

"You look like a cop."

"Trust me, I'm not," I said. "May I come in and ask you a few questions about Arthur?"

"I've already spoken with the police, a horrid FBI agent, and some butch woman from the Nevada Test Site, Mr., Mr.—ah, yes, of course, Mr. Fitzpatrick. Dear Mr. Fitzpatrick."

"Please, call me Frank."

"Because you're so frank, Frank?"

His silliness irritated me. "This is very urgent, Zsa Zsa. Arthur's been gone four days, and his wife is frantic."

The small man closed the door and undid the chain. The door opened, and he stepped out, ornate, scarlet silk kimono flowing around him. He motioned for me to follow, and I stepped into the building. He closed and locked the door behind us. He seemed to glide in his zoris, his small feet encased in thick, fulgent, white socks. Air conditioners roared.

We took the elevator, which he said was causing him occasional trouble, to the top of the building, walked down a long hallway redolent of sandalwood, and entered a room through an ornate, red door that looked as if it had been crafted during the Meiji period.

Scarlet taffeta, in a moiré pattern, adorned the walls of the room. On a red, Victorian sofa lounged three men in their late teens, all of them wearing tight T-shirts and tight blue jeans. The three young men were watching a soap opera and smoking clove cigarettes. On end tables sat several ormolu ashtrays, which overflowed with cigarette butts. The tallest of the young men nodded at me—not with the forehead going down, but with the chin going up—the second ignored me, and the third sneered at me.

"These are my boys," Zsa Zsa said, motioning with a hand. "Aren't they lovely?"

I looked away from the ephebes. "I was hoping that we could speak in private, Zsa Zsa."

"Of course, my dear. Let's talk in my studio."

The studio inhabited a room about thirty feet high and thirty feet wide and a hundred feet long. Acrylic paintings hung on the walls. Several prints of Zsa Zsa's work lay on a table. Zsa Zsa asked if I wanted anything to drink. I said that I was fine. He said that he was going to have tea. His zoris made soft scraping sounds as he moved to a counter littered with boxes of Asian teas.

I wandered from one acrylic painting to the next. Blacks, whites, and reds assaulted my eyes. I was good at semiotics, but I could make no sense of the swirls, numbers, and runes. What did these things mean, if they had any meaning at all? And what did Arthur see in this so-called art?

"Wonderful, aren't they?" Zsa Zsa said, now standing next to me, sipping vanilla tea. He pointed with a pinky. "This is my newest one."

I pointed toward another, smaller painting, which rested on an easel. "I like this one quite a bit. It reminds me of Caillebotte."

"You like that one?"

"Yes, I do," I said. "I'm not a fan of Impressionism, but this one has considerable merit, nonetheless."

"And the others don't?"

"I'm not an art critic," I said, wanting to change the subject.

"You seem to know a lot about art for someone who's not an art critic."

"I'm just familiar with Caillebotte."

"I didn't paint it," Zsa Zsa said, sounding petulant. He moved away from the easel, and I followed, to two red chairs that looked like blobs from a lava lamp. "That was a gift from Jamie, one of my dear, dear friends."

He motioned for me to have a seat in one of the red chairs, which I did. He sat down in the other red chair, kicked off his zoris, and placed his small feet on a red table. The thongs in his zoris had created divots in his fulgent socks between the big toes and the second toes.

"Shoot, my dear. I await your questions eagerly."

"Do you know where Arthur is?"

Zsa Zsa rolled his eyes, looking amused.

"Do you?" I said.

"I've told everyone who has asked me that I don't know. I don't know. I don't know, I don't know, I don't know. Is that sufficient, Frank?"

"Let me start from the beginning, Zsa Zsa, for my own sake. Do you know why he's gone?"

"No, Frank, I don't."

"How did you meet Arthur? Candy says that you're friends, but you don't seem to be the kind of person Arthur would hang around."

"I met Arthur at one of my galleries on the Strip." He made a face, looking like a baby chimp. "I'm not sure which one. It could have been the one at Planet Hollywood, but more than likely it was the smaller one at the Cosmopolitan. Anyway, there I was, having my exhibition and speaking with a duchess from the Netherlands, when Arthur walked up and introduced himself and began asking me questions about my work. You should have seen the look on the duchess's face! Anyway, Arthur's gall—perhaps *cojones* is a better word—intrigued me, and at the time, I just thought he was some eccentric rube tourist who was fortunate enough to have enough brains to get a job as a systems analyst or what have you."

I nodded. "What attracted him to your art?"

"You don't like my art, do you, Frank?"

"No, Zsa Zsa, I don't."

He made a face, which made him look like an irritated squirrel. He sipped his tea, and then he looked up at the ceiling, as if he were contemplating what to say next. He feigned a smile, finished his tea, and placed the porcelain cup on the red table.

"You're very insulting, Frank," he said. "My art earns me millions of dollars a year."

"I'm not saying that it doesn't."

"Eliot Waxwell believes in what I'm doing." Zsa Zsa motioned with his hand, indicating all of his work in the vast interior. "He's my patron. He's a man of wealth and taste. Do you think that you are a man of wealth and taste?"

"I'm not here to talk about your art. I'm here to talk about Arthur."

Zsa Zsa sighed. "I suppose you want to ask me about the argument?"

"Now that you brought it up, yes," I said. "Why did he and Eliot Waxwell have a heated argument?"

"I wouldn't call it that, my dear."

"Candy says that it was a heated argument. Arthur is a very quiet, low-key person. He'll fight, if cornered, but he won't show anger. He showed a lot of anger that night, according to Candy."

"Can you keep a secret?"

"No, but go ahead and tell me anyway, Zsa Zsa."

"Arthur accused Eliot of fraud," the small man said, smiling. His white teeth were like an ermine's. "Of course, that didn't set well with Eliot, who shoved Arthur, after Arthur made the accusation."

"Why did Arthur accuse Eliot Waxwell of fraud?" I said.

"Arthur said that Waxwell had cheated his way to the top. You'll have to ask Arthur about that, if you can find him."

"Some police officers or FBI agents might find that statement highly suspicious."

"Do you, Frank?" He made a face and tilted his head, looking like a questioning dog.

"Not really," I said. "You don't seem to be the threatening type. And Arthur's not the envious type. If he did make that accusation, he was stating it because he believed it to be a fact."

"I would agree."

"Is Arthur one of your patrons?"

"Are you kidding me?" Zsa Zsa said, rolling his eyes. "He doesn't have enough money to be one of my patrons. Any other questions?"

"One that's quite obvious but which few people seem to have asked."

"What is it, Frank?"

"What do you see in Arthur?"

He clapped his hand together and giggled. "I was hoping you were going to ask me that." He sounded like a girl in first grade who was about to share her first big secret with her first best friend. "As Candy probably told you, Arthur entertains at my parties. He's phenomenal. No one can stump him, not even Eliot, and Eliot, mind you, has a mind as sharp as a samurai sword. Mostly, though, and I say this quite honestly, Arthur likes to talk to me about my art. He asks me questions about its meaning and so forth. I find that quite charming."

"But don't you get questions like that all of the time?"

"Mostly superficial ones," Zsa Zsa said. "You see, most of the people who attend my exhibitions are the glitterati. Some of them are exceptionally bright, of course, but most are as stupid as a box of rocks. Arthur genuinely wants to understand my art. He wants to understand what I am saying. *Really* saying."

"What are you saying?"

"Look at my art, and you'll find out."

He stood, indicating that our time together was over. I stood, and Zsa Zsa extended his small hand. I shook it. It felt warm.

"I have much to do now," Zsa Zsa said. "I'm getting ready for a major exhibition in Hong Kong and some horrid black tie event this evening. You do understand, don't you?"

"One quick question, Zsa Zsa."

"What, my dear?"

"Why do you call yourself Zsa Zsa?"

He giggled. "Oh, that. Well, back in Frisco, before I was rich and famous, I used to do drag to earn extra money. How I loved to pose, pose, pose in a blond wig. One time, a cop hassled me and a few of my sisters, and I ended up bitch-slapping him and getting away with it, just as dear old Zsa Zsa did way back when. Hence, the moniker."

"Thank you for your time, Zsa Zsa."

"Have a wonderful day, Frank."

At the Prius, I looked up. At a window in the center of the building, the tallest of the ephebes, the alpha male of the trio, sat, leg dangling, peering down at me. He was smoking a cigarette, which he tapped with an index finger.

"Watch that bike," he said loudly, referring to the black Harley-Davidson, in an accent that hinted of the Deep South. "I paid big bucks for that bike. You touch that bike, I'll touch you."

I shook my head. He thrust out his middle finger at me and called me names and told me to do something to myself that was anatomically impossible.

I got into the Prius and drove toward the highway. Before I took the exit ramp, I called Maxine and told her that I was going to the Nevada Test Site and that she could expect me within the hour.

Three

Maxine was standing next to the badge center. A barrette held her auburn hair in place, and her black, brown, and white dress barely reached her knees. Her silver necklace reflected the August sunlight. Like Candy, Maxine had shapely legs, and, like Candy, Maxine had a bust that caused any straight man with a large breast fetish to salivate. She reminded me of an auburn-haired Jayne Mansfield.

I stopped the car at the badge center and stepped out. Maxine sauntered over, arms out in greeting.

"Long time, Fitz," she said, embracing me. I patted her back, not feeling comfortable. We had been lovers for two months. She had deemed me too cold. I had deemed her too hot. Things had never been quite the same between us. "You're looking better than you ever did."

"Thanks," I said. "You have a visitor's badge for me, Max?"

"Right here," she said, and she handed me badge on a lan-yard, which I donned. "You're only here because I say that you can be here. I just wouldn't do this for anyone, so please, be quiet about it, all right? You said you wanted to see Arthur's office. Is there anything else?"

"That should do," I said, and we walked to the Prius. I opened the door for her, and she slipped into the vehicle and put on her seatbelt. I got into the Prius, closed the door, put on my seatbelt, and started the car, which barely hummed as it came alive. I then drove toward one of the Wackenhut guards at the front gates.

"Any word from the FBI or your people, Max?"

"They were afraid that he might have turned."

"To the Chinese, I suppose?"

"That's right," she said. "But I know Arthur. And Arthur is no traitor."

"I'm surprised that neither you nor your people have any clues."

"Don't be such a smartass, Fitz. I'm not in the mood."

I stopped the vehicle, and a Wackenhut guard, a big-butted behemoth who looked as if he were doing his best to impersonate Rambo, ran his stubby fingers over my temporary badge to ensure that the badge was genuine. Then he meandered around the car, where Maxine rolled down her window, and he did the same thing to her badge. He motioned us on with a flick of his hand. I mock-saluted him. The Wackenhut guard scowled, and I drove through the entrance of the Nevada Test Site, heading toward the administrative buildings. I rolled up the windows. The air conditioning felt light and refreshing.

I parked in the lot of a brown, two-story building. I stared at the building, keeping the engine of the Prius running.

"You all right, Fitz?"

"I wish I weren't here, Max."

"Why?"

"You know what I believe about this place and how I feel about this place."

"Was it so bad here, Fitz?"

"No, it wasn't bad being here, if you're speaking about geography. But if you're speaking about what we were doing here, in terms of our work, then it was bad. It's very disillusioning when you discover that your employer, the government, is run by a group of inept sociopaths, a criminal gang writ large. Sometimes I wonder if I should have remained a Benedictine monk."

She touched my forearm. "I don't think so. You're not the most affectionate guy in the world, but you're also not cut out for celibacy, either."

I turned off the Prius, which went into a deep sleep, and Maxine led the way into the building. The corridor smelled like computer paper and copy machine cartridges. Maxine's high heels click-clacked on the tiled floor.

She unlocked the door to Arthur's office and stepped in and turned on a light. I entered. Certificates and diplomas adorned the walls, as did photographs of Arthur's shaking the hand of the president and the hands of several plenipotentiaries, foreign and domestic. Red tacks and green tacks dotted a planisphere, indicating geographical coordinates of interest. His desk squatted in the center of the room, uncluttered, with everything seemingly in place.

"The FBI took his laptop, of course," Maxine said, closing the door. The fluorescent light overhead snapped, as if irritated at our presence. "They found nothing out of the ordinary on it."

"Have hacking attacks been increasing here at the Site?"

"Of course they've been increasing. Things are especially tense between the US and China right now, you know."

"Oh, I know."

I studied Arthur's bookshelves. Most of the tomes contained abstracts and papers, written by mathematicians working in the field of cyber security. I removed a volume and flipped through it and put it back.

"Are you familiar with Zsa Zsa Cortez?" I said.

"Who?"

"A nonobjective artist whom I find quite objectionable," I said. A wedding photo in the center of a wall showed Arthur—about five-five and bald and bearded and bespectacled—standing beside Candy, each looking lovingly into the other's eyes, each smiling. "Arthur seems to have taken a recent fascination with Zsa Zsa's work, though I don't understand why."

"Never heard of Zsa Zsa Cortez. Besides, Arthur never seemed interested in things like that. It was Candy, work, and mathematics, pretty much in that order."

"Arthur has quite a few photographs here, doesn't he?"

"Yes, I would say that he does."

"They liven up this room, don't they?"

"Yes, they do," Maxine said, sounding a little irritated. "Everyone here has something on their walls. If we didn't, these institutional walls would drive us crazy."

"Why is that?"

"Are you serious?" She made a face, looking like a piqued schoolgirl. "Government offices are boring. B-O-R-I-N-G. Is this the first time that you've noticed that, Fitz?"

I smiled, feeling somewhat rueful. "Yes, I have noticed that. And yes, I am serious. Very serious. Arthur has no prints of the works of Zsa Zsa Cortez, with whose work Arthur is supposed to have become enamored."

I looked away from the photos and at Maxine, who shrugged.

"Could be," she said. "Perhaps there aren't any prints."

"There are. I saw them at Zsa Zsa Cortez's studio."

"Perhaps you should ask her, Fitz."

"Him," I said, correcting Maxine. "His real name's Enrique."

Maxine bit the corner of her mouth, then released the corner of her mouth. The pink gloss on her lips made them look shiny, especially under the fluorescent lighting.

"What do you think happened to Arthur?" she said.

"You first, Max. What do you think happened?"

"I don't know, Fitz."

"Neither do I."

I asked if I could examine the contents of his desk, and Maxine unlocked the desk drawers, which I went through. I then examined Arthur's file cabinet, in which I found nothing unusual.

It was getting close to noon. Maxine asked if I wanted to eat lunch. I said that sounded like a good idea. We left the administrative building and walked to a cafeteria two blocks away. During lunch, Maxine and I talked about the investigation into Arthur's disappearance. The investigation seemed to be going nowhere, and Maxine seemed very frustrated by that. Around us, Test Site employees, the ones who worked beyond the standard Monday through Thursday shifts, talked about their families or the upcoming weekend.

After lunch, Maxine and I went to the Prius. Maxine asked me if I wanted to go on a few rounds with her. We could catch up on old times, she said. I declined. She embraced me and kissed my cheek. I blushed. Maxine chuckled.

"You were never one for PDAs, Fitz, but I tell you, you should be. You are still one hot man."

"Thanks," I said, patting my paunch. "But I don't think that you noticed this."

"Better watch myself, I guess. You could turn me in for sexual harassment."

"Don't worry about that, Max. I'm not politically correct. Talk with you soon. And, oh, if you find out anything about Arthur, please call me before you speak with Candy, all right? She's fragile. I don't want anything to shatter her."

Maxine nodded. I got into the Prius, backed it out of the parking lot, and headed to the front gates, where I turned in my visitor's badge to the heavy-bottomed Rambo, who scowled when I mock-saluted him before heading down the highway leading back to Las Vegas.

Four

I stopped at a Subway in North Las Vegas, where I called Candy on my cell phone, telling her that I would be back later that day. I then pulled up a Google browser on my cell phone, entered the keywords ZSA ZSA CORTEZ GALLERIES LAS VEGAS, and found three galleries in Las Vegas that sold his work. The largest of the galleries, according to the search, was at the Miracle Mile Shops at the Planet Hollywood Casino. So, off to the Planet Hollywood Casino I went.

Tourists hurried about and within the casino. Men and women sold chilled bottles of water out on the sidewalks. I headed into the Miracle Mile Shops.

Inside, I asked a concierge where I could find the Jacobs Gallery. She unfolded a map, circled a store on the map with a red pen, and handed the map to me. I thanked her for her time. She feigned a smile, and I proceeded farther into the artificial world of the Miracle Mile Shops.

The labyrinthine passageway seemed as if it was never going to end, and I wondered if I was going to encounter the Minotaur. Instead, I encountered tourists meandering from shop to shop. At a table near one of the shops, a tarot card reader read for an elderly woman, who kept demanding to know, in a loud voice that carried throughout the passageway, if Irving was going to come back to her and what the winning numbers of the lotto were.

I continued, following the map that the concierge had given to me. The Jacobs Gallery appeared at the end of the passageway. Paintings by Zsa Zsa Cortez hung in the windows. I paused to look at them, read a bio ("Born in Cebu City and raised in San Francisco, Enrique 'Zsa Zsa' Cortez became a noted child prodigy in the art world there, entering the San Francisco Art Institute at the age of twelve…"), then entered the gallery.

A woman, sitting at a desk set as high as a judge's, looked up from a copybook into which she had been writing sinistrally. Her cheeks and nose and chin and eyebrows were angular. Though she could not have been more than thirty, she was wearing black reading glasses—the nosepiece of which rested upon the tip of her vulpine nose—that would have been more at home on a septuagenarian. Her thick, henna-colored hair was pulled back in a tight bun, making her look like an old-time spinster. Her hands were fine, resembling a porcelain doll's, and her nails were clipped and painted bright red. She blinked.

"Yes?" she said. "How may I help you?"

"May I ask you a few questions about the work of Zsa Zsa Cortez?"

"Very good," she said, and she stood up from the desk and descended three steps that led to a tessellated floor. She removed her reading glasses, which were connected to a chain around her neck, and let the reading glasses rest on her narrow chest. Her perfume smelled like a light, vanilla spritz. "He's our best-selling painter. He's a mathematical genius. His work has covered everything from the Fibonacci sequence to the minutiae of quantum mechanics. Are you familiar with his new series?" Then she blinked, as if caught off-guard by something. "Oh, pardon me. Forgive me for not introducing myself. I'm Marie LeBeau, the gallery manager."

"And I'm Frank Fitzpatrick. And no, I'm not familiar with the series."

"You sound very interested in Zsa Zsa Cortez's work."

"Not really," I said. "In fact, I'm not sure why anyone would want to buy it."

She blinked. From the expression on her face, she either thought that I was crazy or playing some sort of practical joke on her. She looked around the gallery, as if expecting to see a candid camera crew hunkering down with camcorders and microphones.

"Pardon me?" She turned her face so that it was sideways to me. "You said that you were interested in his work."

"Not in the work, *per se*, but in questions about it," I said. "For starters, why does he have such a following?"

"His new lithographic series just came out," she said, not seeming to want to answer my question. "I'd be glad to show you the series. If you're interested in one of the lithographs or more, I can show—"

"I won't be purchasing any of his artwork. Ever."

"Then why are you asking me about his work?"

I offered her a hundred dollar bill. She peered at it.

"This is yours," I said, "if you'll answer a few questions. I won't be here longer than ten minutes. This bill will more than adequately pay for your time."

"Move over slightly to the left, out of the way of the security camera."

I did, and she took the bill and pocketed it somewhere on her black dress. "All right, what would you like to know about his work, Mr. Fitzpatrick?"

"I'm trying my best to understand why anyone would want to purchase it. I can see someone's wanting to purchase a Michelangelo or a da Vinci or a Rembrandt or a Wyeth or a Hopper. These are great painters. I know that people buy the works of Picasso and Pollock and other artists like them because of the publicity associated with their names and not the quality of work, which is nonexistent. But even Zsa Zsa Cortez's work doesn't compare to Picasso's or Pollock's. Why is Zsa Zsa Cortez's work popular?"

The gallery manager sighed. "I know why, but I'm not sure if I can tell you why."

"Why not?"

"Because if I told you the reason—the real reason—I could get fired."

"I promise not to say a word."

"You look like someone who keeps promises."

"Promises, yes, secrets, no," I said.

She chuckled and crossed her arms. "The truth is, Zsa Zsa Cortez became famous because of Eliot Waxwell. Eliot Waxwell promotes Zsa Zsa among the glitterati, especially the Kardashians and their new rivals, the Ryersons. It's the 'emperor's new clothes,' but no one has figured out that they're the emperor."

"How true," I said. "So, what does Eliot Waxwell see in his work?"

"You've got me," the gallery manager said. "But Mr. Jacobs— he owns the gallery—he insists that we carry the work. It sells because of Zsa Zsa's appearances in all those reality television shows. He's way over the top, you know."

"Oh, I know. I met him earlier today."

"You met Zsa Zsa Cortez?" she said, sounding impressed. "How did you manage that?"

"One of my old friends is seemingly a devotee of his work. His wife knows Zsa Zsa and has been to his studio. She gave me the address, and I drove there this morning."

She uncrossed her arms. "So, why does your friend like Zsa Zsa Cortez's work?"

I walked over to one of Zsa Zsa's paintings—blobs of red, white, and black acrylic crisscrossing a canvas—and I shook my head.

"I don't know," I said. "And to be honest, I can't really say if Arthur, my friend, likes the work or is merely interested in it. Just because someone is interested in something doesn't mean that they like it."

"Here's a question that just came to mind," she said. "Why don't you ask him?"

I turned to her. "Because he's been missing since this past Monday evening. I'm not sure, but I think Zsa Zsa Cortez and his art might have something to do with it."

"It's not that scientist from the Test Site, is it?" she said. Her vulpine nose twitched. "There's a big hunt out for him."

"He's a mathematician, to get technical. And so I've seen."

We were silent a few moments.

"Excuse me, but I must get back to work," she said, and she ascended the three steps to her desk, putting her reading glasses back on. "Mr. Jacobs is hosting a party for the mayor and for some Chinese officials. We're showcasing Zsa Zsa Cortez's work. He's going to be there. Eliot Waxwell is slated to be there, too."

"Is the party open to the public or at a public venue?" I said.

She shook her head. "No, the party's not."

"I suppose that Mr. Jacobs is hosting the party somewhere in Las Vegas." I removed two one hundred dollar bills from my wallet. "Will these purchase me a MapQuest?"

Marie LeBeau smiled. She generated a map for me, I slid the bills to her out of sight of the security camera, and she told me it was a black tie event and that I should be dressed accordingly. I thanked her for her time and left the gallery and entered the labyrinthine passageway of the Miracle Mile Shops.

Five

Candy had a black dress and a pair of black high heels perfect for that evening's black tie event. I, on the other hand, had come to Las Vegas with loose-fitting shirts, slightly baggy slacks, ratty shorts, and a pair of Converse sneakers. After dinner, Candy and I went to a men's discount clothing store in Summerlin, where I tried on three tuxedos before renting the first one. I purchased a pair of black socks and a pair of black shoes to go along with the tuxedo. By the time Candy and I were done, it was getting dark. She drove us in her Mercedes to the Jacobs residence. We found a parking space half a block away.

Latino servers walked to the front gate of the Jacobs residence, wearing white jackets and black slacks and red ties and black shoes. The shoes were so highly polished that even under sodium-vapor light, the shoes shone brilliantly, as if under the sun. Two of the servers were speaking in bracero Spanish, joking about the white, fancy, rich gringos whom the servers would be serving that evening.

Candy rested her hand in the crook of my arm, and we walked toward the gate that the Latino servers had passed through. Her black dress contoured her shapely figure nicely. I did my best not to stare at her Monroesque cleavage.

"I feel like I'm sneaking into a movie theater," she said.

"Just a like a kid, huh?"

"No, not just like a kid, Frank. I feel like we're going to get caught." A beat. "I'm scared."

"Trust me, we're not going to get caught. Everything's going to be fine, Candy."

"How can you be so sure?"

"Because we have an ally in there."

A man, looking like a paladin at Charlemagne's court, stood at the front door, taking invitations from people and then nodding, allowing people to enter the party. Candy and I approached.

"Invitation?" he said, and from his accent, I could tell that he was from the Midlands of England.

"We don't have one," I said. "But one of your guests will vouch for us."

"Oh? Who?"

"The man of the hour, Zsa Zsa Cortez," I said. "Please send someone to find Mr. Cortez, and tell him that Frank Fitzpatrick and Candy Vogel are here to see him."

The man spoke into a microphone that he held in his right hand. There was the squawk of static, and a few seconds later, Zsa Zsa Cortez appeared at the door.

"Oh, my, you are something else, aren't you?" he said, giggling. Like me, Zsa Zsa was wearing a tuxedo. Unlike me, Zsa Zsa was wearing a neon pink cummerbund and a bowtie of the same color. "What are you two lovelies doing here?"

From the way that he slurred when he stepped forward to embrace Candy, I knew that the painter was drunk. I shook hands with the effeminate little man and motioned for him to lead us into the party, which he did. Candy raised an eyebrow. I nodded in acknowledgement—yes, we were in.

Zsa Zsa ambled, stumbling every third or fourth step in the magnificent hallway.

"I didn't know if I would ever see you again, Frank," Zsa Zsa said, looking and sounding rueful. "Did you miss me? Is this why you're here at the party?"

"No, I didn't miss you," I said, and he pouted. "The truth is, Zsa Zsa, Candy and I are still searching for Arthur Vogel."

"And you think"—and he hiccoughed here—"and you think that he's somewhere here?"

"No, but if he is, it would be great to find him, Zsa Zsa. I'm hoping that, perhaps, I can learn more information about his recent whereabouts from attendees."

He pouted. "You mean you want to speak to Eliot, don't you? You didn't come here because of me or my work. You came here because of Eliot Waxwell."

"And any others who might have the information that we need," I said.

Candy walked on the other side of Zsa Zsa.

"Where is he?" she said. She grabbed Zsa Zsa and shook him. His head bounced back and forth, and he reminded me of a mechanical monkey that I had owned when I was a child. "What did you do with Arthur?"

I stepped between the two of them and separated them. Candy's cheeks had turned a bright red. Zsa Zsa leaned against a wall, holding himself up on an ornate table. His eyes watered, and he wagged a finger at Candy.

"Don't you ever, ever touch me," he said, and now he didn't sound so drunk, but because he was bobbing and weaving on his feet, I knew that he was. "Don't you agree, Frank? Don't you agree that she shouldn't touch me?"

"I agree, Zsa Zsa," I said and made a pretense of smoothing the sleeves of his elegant tuxedo jacket. "Now, if you'd lead us to the party and introduce us, we would greatly appreciate it."

"Oh, yes," and he giggled. "Of course. The party. How can we forget the party?"

The party, which was composed of two hundred or so people, filled a huge ballroom at the center of the expansive house. Zsa Zsa's paintings stood on easels or hung suspended from a high ceiling. Latino servers moved about, offering flutes of champagne and hors d'oeuvres to guests. Zsa Zsa introduced us to art critics from New York City, a rancher from New Mexico who had started investing in fine art, and the head of a London bank, a viscount whose expression clearly showed that he was bored and that he didn't want to be at the party. We passed Oscar Goodman, Las Vegas's most notorious ex-mayor. He had a clear drink in his hand and raised the drink and saluted me when he and I made eye contact. A trio—standup bass, guitar, and drums—in the center of the ballroom made offbeat, cacophonous sounds.

Zsa Zsa led me by the arm to a group of Chinese men who were standing in a circle, holding flutes of champagne in front of their chests and chatting amiably one with one another in Cantonese. Zsa Zsa attempted to speak in Cantonese, but the men shook their heads, making it clear that they didn't understand what he was saying. Two of the men chuckled, and one with a facial scar, which was shaped like the east coast of South America and which ran from the corner of his left eye to the corner of his small mouth, scowled. Zsa Zsa pointed at Candy and me, and one of the men—clearly the group's leader—extended his hand.

"Wang Min," he said. "I'm the CEO of Fookien."

"Hanjin's biggest competitor," I said, shaking his hand, which had a tight grip. From the way he spoke English, I could tell that he had spent time in England, perhaps at Oxford or Cambridge. "I've read about you. I'm Frank Fitzpatrick, and this is my companion, Candy Vogel."

The man shook Candy's hand and bowed simultaneously. Candy didn't bow.

"I've purchased several of Mr. Cortez's pieces," the shipping magnate said, releasing Candy's hand and turning to me. "Have you ever seen anything like them, Mr. Fitzpatrick?"

"Quite frankly, no, I haven't. May I ask why you invested in them?"

"Of course," he said, and now the other Chinese gentlemen had formed another circle of their own. Candy stood on my right, Zsa Zsa on my left. "Mr. Cortez's work shows the mixing of the objective with the nonobjective. Or, in other words, they are the blending of reality with non-reality. They express, in substance, the balancing of the energies in our universe, unlike what any other artist has ever done. When I saw Mr. Cortez's paintings, I knew that I had to have them for my casino in Macao."

"Don't forget your home," Zsa Zsa said, giggling. "You've contracted me to complete a series of murals, much in the way Peggy Guggenheim contracted Jackson Pollock."

"That is correct," said Wang, who smiled widely, showing teeth that had been bleached bone white. "Mr. Cortez will be coming over to Macao to work on the commission sometime later this year."

"Oh, call me Zsa Zsa," the little man said, and he waved a hand at the shipping magnate and then touched the magnate's hand, as if Zsa Zsa and the magnate were going steady in high school. "Why must you always be so formal, Michael?" Zsa Zsa looked at me. "Michael is his English name. I bet you didn't know that, Frank."

The shipping magnate chuckled and removed his hand from Zsa Zsa's clasp. The magnate smiled at Zsa Zsa, but I knew that the smile was a pretense: the magnate hated the effeminate man. I could tell by the magnate's stiff posture when Zsa Zsa touched him, clearly showing repulsion. Other indicators included the cinching of the magnate's pupils, as if suddenly exposed to a bright, distasteful light, and the fine, dark hairs on the sides of the magnate's neck standing at attention.

Zsa Zsa smiled, completely unaware of the shipping magnate's true feelings.

Wang looked at me. I knew that he did not like me. And he knew that I did not like him.

"If you'll excuse me," he said, turning, leaving us.

"And you think you know something about art," Zsa Zsa said, peering up at me. "Well, you don't know anything, Frank. What do you think about that?"

"I think it's time for us to get a drink," I said to Candy, taking her hand. "We'll talk to you later, Zsa Zsa." Candy and I walked toward a bar, behind which stood a dour-faced bartender, the sole white among the servers. The furrows on his brow grew deeper when he saw us, and I studied his browned and spotted face, which had obviously been exposed to too much sun. "Zsa Zsa was beginning to get on my nerves."

"One more minute, and I would have blown up," Candy said. I ordered Perrier water on the rocks, and Candy ordered a dirty martini. The bartender made our drinks without acknowledging us. "He's the most arrogant little man that I've ever met."

"I've met plenty in my lifetime," I said. Then I saw the man for whom I'd been looking. "There he is."

"Eliot Waxwell?"

"The one and only."

A group of hoydens, wearing too-tight-fitting dresses and high heels, had encircled Waxwell, who was speaking animatedly and gesticulating. The young women laughed.

The bartender handed Candy her dirty martini and handed me my Perrier water. I tipped him and motioned with a nod of my head, indicating for Candy to follow me.

"What are you going to say to him?" Candy said as we made our way toward Waxwell's group.

"I'll know when I get there."

One of the young women was still laughing heartily, and another young woman nudged the laughing woman, indicating that she should stop laughing. The laughing young woman apologized and laughed again. The young woman who had done the nudging snorted, then laughed. And now the other young women laughed. Eliot Waxwell smiled like a proud sultan lording over his harem.

"Mr. Waxwell?" I said.

Two burly bruiser boys stepped forward.

Waxwell turned to me, but he didn't answer.

"I believe that you know my companion, Candy Vogel," I said. "I'm Frank Fitzpatrick, a friend of Arthur Vogel. I was wondering if I could ask you a few questions about Arthur."

"Oh?" Eliot Waxwell smirked. "What kind of questions?"

"Questions that might get you off the hook, Mr. Waxwell."

His eyes became thin slits. His nostrils flared.

"May I have a moment with you in private, Mr. Waxwell?"

He nodded at the bodyguards, and I looked at Candy, telling her silently that she was to stay behind. Waxwell told the women that he would be back in a few moments. He and I walked toward a dark, solitary corner of the ballroom.

His cologne—I was never good at discerning colognes—smelled expensive. His thick, black, curly hair hung over an eye. He walked with his head slightly tilted back and to the side. He came off as an arrogant street punk with the swagger of a Western gunslinger. As we walked, people parted the way for him.

"I barely know Arthur Vogel," he said, "and I don't know what happened to Arthur Vogel. I've already talked with the cops and the feds—"

"I'm not a cop, and I'm not a fed, Mr. Waxwell. I'll be clear and upfront about that."

"So, what's all this about getting me off the hook?"

"My apologies," I said. "It was bait to get you alone."

"Are you really a friend of Arthur Vogel, Frank?"

"More of an acquaintance now, truth be told. I used to live here, in Las Vegas, where I worked with Arthur. We were good friends, until I made a decision that caused a rift between us. It seems that you and Arthur Vogel might have a rift between the two of you, too."

Waxwell sipped his drink. "Why should I speak to you, Frank?"

"There's nothing that says that you should, Mr. Waxwell."

"Are you a private detective?"

"Something like that," I said. "I'm not sure how you would define it. I work for friends or when someone in dire need requires my services. Sometimes I get paid, sometimes I don't. It depends upon the situation."

"Friends like Arthur Vogel?"

"Yes, and Candy Vogel, his wife. What's interesting is that you say that you barely know Arthur, yet he got into a heated argument with you at one of Zsa Zsa Cortez's parties. Civilized people who barely know each other typically don't get into arguments like that."

"I don't know what his problem was," Waxwell said. "As far as I know, he's some genius of a mathematician who took a liking to Zsa Zsa's art. Maybe he was drunk or on drugs."

I looked from the corner of my eye. Candy was sitting at a table, dirty martini in hand, looking in our direction. Oscar Goodman stood next to the head of the London bank, the viscount. Goodman laughed. The viscount looked stiff and bored.

"Arthur doesn't get drunk," I said. "And he doesn't do drugs, unless they're prescription ones, and at the time, I don't believe that he was on anything that would cause him to have that sort of public outburst. Would you please tell me what the argument was about?"

Waxwell finished his champagne. "It was about nothing. Nothing. Nada. Zilch."

"Please humor me, Mr. Waxwell," I said. "I could use a good joke."

"I bet you could, Frank." He sounded menacing, and he sounded mean.

I stared back, not blinking, not flinching. A few moments passed. Then he blinked.

He placed the empty flute onto a table and leaned back against the table, crossing his arms. He stared across the room, at an elegant elderly woman with bouffant blond hair. Waxwell looked like a wolf sizing up its prey.

"Arthur Vogel," and now Waxwell looked at me, "says that I became rich because I cheated people. If anyone knows my story, that's not the case. I started off poor in northern Florida, all right, but I was smart, and I used my smarts in the oil business, starting in Oklahoma and then overseas, in the Middle East and then in Africa. I learned quickly, and I learned good, believe you me. I could go on about my investments in Peruvian mines and how well I've done in the Forex and commodities markets and how I broke into the casino racket, but I won't bore you with the details. It's enough to say that I didn't have to cheat anyone to make my billions, that's for sure."

"Then why did Arthur accuse you of that?" I said. "It's not like him."

"Probably because of something that Zsa Zsa said."

"What was that?"

"I overhead the little queer," Waxwell said, sneering. Then he guffawed like a good old boy. "Go ahead and tell that little queer that I called him a little queer, if you want. What's he going to do?"

"Why should I tell him that you called him that? What good would it do?"

Waxwell snorted. "Nothing. Never mind."

"So, what exactly did Zsa Zsa say?"

"That I pulled off the greatest fraud in the world by promoting his work," Waxwell said, and he nodded, indicating a buxom woman in a red dress who walked past us. "See, Zsa Zsa knows that what he does isn't real art. Why do you think he's drunk tonight? He knows he's a fake, and he can't face that. Little queer, he thinks he's some sort of genius, though. When I found him, he was doing contract work as an interior decorator at one of my gigs here in Vegas. Claimed he could create these far-out paintings no one had ever seen the likes of. So, I asked to see, and he showed me pictures on his cell phone of this so-called great art, and after I looked at it, I knew I had a way to get my revenge."

"Revenge? Revenge against whom, Mr. Waxwell?"

"Who else?" he said, uncrossing his arms and holding them out, indicating the entire ballroom. "Las Vegas. And the other bastards who said that I don't belong here or anywhere else. Those New England bluebloods, they think they own everything. They think they can run everything. They think they call tell someone where they belong or don't belong. Well, I decided to show them what kind of idiots they really are. Jacobs was doing poorly in his business, but I got him to buy a whole bunch of Zsa Zsa's crap. Then I got my PR people to jump on it, and before you know it, those bluebloods were paying boocoo bucks for stuff that any chimp could've painted."

"You showed them, didn't you?"

"Hell if I didn't." Waxwell winked. "I can tell that you and me are a lot alike, Frank. You hate them too. I can tell."

I felt contempt for celebrities the way that he felt contempt for the superrich elite, who wanted to exclude him from their world. Yet, Waxwell's reason for promoting Zsa Zsa's work would not have caused Arthur to become so angry.

"Gotta go," Waxwell said, and he punched me lightly in the arm and then absent-mindedly handed me one of his business cards. "Bitches are waiting. I'm going to have at least two to-night. I'd give you one, but it looks like you have your hands full already."

"Why—"

"Later."

And Waxwell walked away, disappearing among the guests in the ballroom.

Candy touched the back of my arm. "Find out anything that might be useful, Frank?"

"Nothing," I said, shaking my head and putting Waxwell's business card into my wallet. "I think we're done here, unless you want to stay."

"No, I want to get out of this place."

On the way out, Candy and I said goodbye to Zsa Zsa, who, in his drunkenness, had forgotten that we were there. Mrs. Jacobs said that she hoped that Candy and I had enjoyed ourselves at the party. I said that Candy and I had had a lovely time. Mrs. Jacobs beamed, and Candy and I headed toward the front door.

Six

Several ground lights illuminated the palatial estate, making the estate look like Las Vegas's tribute to the Taj Mahal. I held Candy's hand in the crook of my arm, and we went through the front gate and walked to the Mercedes. Moths flittered around a streetlight, and a bird swooped in, eating the moths. In the distance, on the Strip, the beam of a searchlight explored the sky. An ambulance siren wailed somewhere. The August night felt hot. I wanted to get back to Candy's, get out of the tux and out of the dress shoes, and then take a long, cold shower.

Candy stepped off the curb, and when she did, the lights on a car about one hundred feet away came on.

"I think that I should drive," I said, walking around the Mercedes.

"I'm perfectly capable of driving, Frank."

"Candy, don't turn your head, but I think we're going to be followed. Please, let me drive."

She nodded and handed me the keys.

After we got in, I fired up the ignition of the Mercedes. I pulled the car away from the curb.

Candy looked over her shoulder. "Is that the car?"

I nodded. "That's the car."

I drove up the street at the legal limit. The car sped up to us, too close for comfort. If I had slammed on the brakes, the tailing car would have rammed us.

"I don't like this, Frank."

"Neither do I, Candy. But let's play it cool. If it is who I think it is, we'll be all right."

I turned on the signal, indicating that we were going to turn left onto another residential street, which contained other estates similar to the Jacobs residence, only about half the size. The car followed us. I increased my speed. The car increased its speed. I made sure, however, that I drove at the legal limit.

"What's going on?" Candy said.

"We'll be all right. You'll see."

And, just as I had expected, I looked up into the rearview mirror and saw blue lights and red lights flashing from the unmarked police vehicle. I drove the Mercedes to a curb.

"You don't have to offer any identification because you're a passenger," I said. "So, if you're asked for it, don't show it. And don't say a word, even if they become threatening. Follow my lead, Candy."

Two men stepped out of the unmarked vehicle and headed toward the Mercedes, one on Candy's side of the vehicle, one on mine. I rolled down my window about an inch and waited. A flashlight beam searched the interior of the Mercedes. I stared ahead.

"Roll down your window," the cop said.

"You should know better, Mankowski," I said. I turned my head slightly, just enough to see his outline. "You tried this last time, and it didn't work."

His partner made a sound like a grunt and a nervous laugh at the same time. Mankowski breathed heavily, as if he'd been running a long-distance race.

"Out of the car," he said. "I can't see your hands. And your friend, too."

Candy and I stepped out of the Mercedes. Mankowski shined the flashlight directly into my face.

"What are you doing back in Vegas, Fitzpatrick?"

"We invoke our Fifth Amendment rights and refuse to answer any questions."

Mankowski lowered the flashlight. Streetlight illuminated him. His suit looked neat and immaculate, the way any detective's suit should look. And his black shoes were shiny but not honed to perfection, the way the Latino servers' had been. One of his bulging eyes looked off-center, and his chin and forehead were bony, like a Neanderthal's. Since I had last seen him, his hairline had receded farther, and he resembled an ugly, overgrown baby with wisps of blond hair and burnsides. A light wend blew, and I caught a whiff of stale cigarette smoke—Merits. While I typically don't like to compare humans to animals, fish, or reptiles—it inexorably insults the creature—Mankowski would have made a good iguana, which, in its stupidity, stares for hours at nothing.

"Want me to search the car?" his partner said. The partner looked like a kid fresh out of high school—a few pimples on his nose and cheeks and gangly in a teenage sort of way in his ill-fitting suit. His stylized hair shined under the street light, as if coated with shellac.

"We invoke our Fourth Amendment rights, Junior," I said to the partner.

Mankowski made a sound like a gasp, not quite a gasp, but something like it.

"You ain't welcome in this town, Fitzpatrick. I got word of what you're doing here, and I don't like it. It's our job, not yours, to find that physician."

"Mathematician," I said, correcting him. "Are we being detained, or are we free to go?"

Mankowski's partner demanded to see Candy's identification. She didn't say anything or move. The gangly cop demanded her ID once again.

"She doesn't have to show you anything," I said. "She's a passenger. You know the law. Or should."

"I thought you were invoking your First Amendment rights," Mankowski said.

"You mean Fourth Amendment rights," I said. "And, yes, I am invoking them, and I am invoking our Fifth Amendment rights, too, as well as our other constitutional rights. Are we being detained, or are we free to go?"

Mankowski cussed and motioned for his partner to leave Candy alone, which Mankowski's partner did. Mankowski and his partner walked back to the unmarked patrol car, its blue lights and red lights flashing. Mankowski said that I had better watch my step. He said that he would be watching me. He said that I had no right to return to Las Vegas. And he said that I had better not screw up—not in those exact terms but close enough—or he would be all over me like honey on flies.

Mankowski and his partner got into the unmarked patrol car and drove away, the blue lights and red lights off, tires screeching as the car sped off somewhere into the Las Vegas night.

"Honey on flies?" Candy said. "He can't be that stupid."

"He is. All police departments have their fair share of dolts on the force, but Mankowski takes the cake. Besides being full of malapropisms, amphibolies, and other verbal atrocities of the mentally deficient, he's living proof that the Peter Principle should be called the Peter Law."

"What was that all about, Frank?"

"Let's go find a place and get a drink to settle your nerves. I'll tell you there."

Candy's GPS directed us, in a stentorian, English-accented voice, to the Vesuvio, a wine bar a few blocks away. We took a corner table. Candy was shaking, and I reached across the table and placed my hand on hers. She looked as if she were going to cry.

"After Arthur and I had our falling out, and after you and Arthur left for Baltimore, I got involved in a case involving a couple of Mankowski's good friends," I said. "They were detectives, working on a crack-related murder on Fremont Street. They found a homeless drunk, whom they believed to be the perp. During the interrogation, they shook the drunk violently, and he vomited on one of them. The two poltroons went into a frenzy and ended up beating the homeless man senseless. He lapsed into a coma and died two days later.

"Las Vegas PD did its best to cover it up, of course. The top cops said that the beating was justified because the man had attacked the two cops during the interrogation. Many people disbelieved the story, and the man's relatives were among them. They hired me to look into the case, which I did. To make a long story short, I saw to it that Mankowski's friends got stints in prison. And I almost got Mankowski thrown off the force for obstruction of justice. Mankowski made it clear that I wasn't wanted in Las Vegas." A beat. "So did a lot of other cops."

"Is that why you moved down to Florida, Frank?"

"It was one of the reasons," I said. "That, and I like the beaches and the ocean down there. To me, these things affirm one of my dearest values—life."

She smiled. A waiter, a man with cropped, brown hair and an acne-scarred face, came to take our order. Candy ordered a glass of Merlot, and I ordered a decaf coffee. He commented on how well-dressed we were and glanced one too many times at Candy's ample cleavage. I frowned at the waiter, who, upon seeing my

frown, looked nervous and hurried off, saying that he would return with our drinks.

"How did he know that we were there, Frank?"

"They had someone at the party who tipped them off," I said.
"More than likely, it was that bartender."

"How can you be so sure?"

"Because he was the only white among the servers, who were all
Latino," I said. "He probably called Mankowski while I was talking to
Eliot Waxwell. Of course, this indicates something far more telling."

"Like what?"

"That the police believe that someone at the party is involved
in Arthur's disappearance," I said. "And that they're taking his
disappearance very, very seriously."

The waiter brought our drinks. He smiled at Candy and made
small talk, complimenting us once again on how we looked that
evening. I watched his eyes, which darted every now and then to
Candy's Monroesque cleavage. I knew what he was thinking. He
asked if we were locals, and before Candy could answer, I said
that we were not and that we wanted to have some privacy. The
waiter smiled the way a man of weak character smiled and excused himself.

"Is this doing any good?" Candy said, after he went away.

"What do you mean?"

"We're not finding Arthur," she said, aspirating. "I feel so
damn guilty going to a party—"

"We weren't just going to a party," I said. "We were looking for
leads. As I said last night, we have to remain calm, and we have
to remain focused. And we have to avoid doing stupid things like
driving around Las Vegas and the desert all night, hoping that
we'll find Arthur."

She bit the corner of her mouth. "You don't believe he's alive,
do you?" Tears welled up in her eyes. I reached over with a cloth
napkin and wiped the tears away.

"I don't know what to believe," I said, dabbing. "I'm gathering
information, and the more I gather, the more the facts are going
to fall into place. Believe me, Arthur just didn't disappear. He's
out there somewhere. As I said, I'm going to do my best to find
him. But to do that, I must take a logical approach. And, so far,
that's what I've been doing."

Candy nodded. We finished our drinks, I paid at the front register, and we left the wine bar and its lecherous waiter behind us.

I drove us back to Summerlin. Candy and I were silent. Many cars sped up and down Lake Mead Boulevard, but when Candy and I neared Summerlin, the traffic became sparse, and there were fewer and fewer street lights. We drove past two-story houses, many of them having palm trees in the front yard. In a way, it was like being back in Florida.

Back at the house, Candy kicked off her high heels, removed her nylons, and said that her feet—one of which she massaged with her hands—were killing her. I sat down on the sofa and undid my tie, tired of the tux and tired of the fancy shoes that pinched my big toes. I asked her if she wanted to watch the news, and she said no. She said that she was going to bed, kissed me on the cheek, and told me goodnight.

I watched the news, but no mention was made about Arthur, and the talking head, a woman barely twenty-one, if that, said that the channel was going to present a three-part series that coming week about the exponentially growing flow of heroin and other drugs into the Southwest.

After turning off the television set, I went upstairs to the guest bedroom, got out of my clothes, and showered. After I toweled myself dry, I put on a Bermuda shirt and a ratty pair of shorts. My cell phone rang.

"Fitz?" Maxine said. She sounded exasperated or nervous, perhaps both.

"What is it, Max?"

"They found him."

I held my breath, then exhaled. I sat down on the bed. My hands felt cold, and my mouth felt dry. I licked my dry lips. My temples thumped. I lay back on the bed.

"You there, Fitz?"

"Where did they find him, Max?"

She gave me directions, which I wrote down on a pad after forcing myself to sit up. I told Maxine that I would be there in half an hour or so.

"Are you going to tell her now?" Maxine said.

"I'll tell her later," I said. "I'll see you in a bit."

Seven

I left Summerlin and took the highway down to the Strip. On the Strip, I saw thousands of motley attired tourists meandering from one casino to the next. On a corner, in front of a Harley-Davidson store, a soon-to-be bride simulated stand-up copulation with a man, while women in her bachelorette party watched.

From the Strip, I drove to the middle of Harmon Avenue and parked across from an abandoned apartment complex. A ten-foot-high, concertina-wire-topped fence surrounded the complex, indicating that the place was marked for demolition. DANGER —DO NOT ENTER signs appeared every teen feet or so on the fence. Police cars with flashing lights had encircled the block. People crossed the street to join groups of other people, who had gathered at the fence, obviously wanting to see what had happened.

I stepped out of the car. Down the street stood the Hard Rock Hotel and Casino. A light breeze caressed my face, and I smelled hamburgers and French fries from a nearby twenty-four-hour grill. I crossed the street, where a group of people had gathered at a gate. A television journalist was interviewing a cop, who was speaking loudly and gesturing with one hand, the other hand in his pocket.

Maxine, who was standing near the gate, waved at me. A barrette held her hair in place, and she was wearing a beige suit, looking as if she was ready for work Monday morning. I walked toward her, my Converses crunching gravel. A cop stepped in my way to block me, holding out a beefy mitt, telling me that I wasn't allowed onto the crime scene. Maxine flashed her badge and said that my presence was authorized. The cop raised an eyebrow, made a face, and stormed off like pouting child denied an extra dessert.

I knew the place. It was an old motel that had been fashioned to resemble a pirate's cove. Someone could have turned the place into a historical landmark, but the old motel had been converted into apartments for the not-so-savory denizens of Las Vegas's underbelly. Several vacated, two-story buildings littered the grounds, along with debris that desert winds had blown in. Palm trees among the buildings hung limp, dying from not having been watered. The air smelled like burned twitch.

"They're getting ready to demolish this sty," Maxine said, leading the way. "And it's about time. This was a hot spot for crack and other illegal drugs for a numbers of years. But we're not here because of this place's lurid past, are we?"

"Who found Arthur? And where?"

"A security guard who's been patrolling the grounds to keep the transients and druggies out. He found Arthur's body in one of the laundry rooms. It's near the swimming pool. He recognized Arthur because of all of the news reports."

We waited outside the gutted laundry room, not saying anything, while crime scene investigators worked. From the light of the night sky, I saw glimmering, slimy water in an abandoned pool. Someone had designed the pool to look like a tropical island, dotted with small mountains and surrounded by a moat. I imagined a family from Texas—heavyset dad, sporting glasses and a crew cut and a gaudy Hawaiian shirt, homemaker mom with bouffant hair, and three children with freckle-splattered faces—hanging out at the pool, circa 1962. And I imagined teenagers hanging out at the pool, sunbathing and wolfing down cheeseburgers and sipping vanilla milkshakes and chasing one another, laughing in the misspent joy of youth. Not one of them—no, not the teenagers, and certainly not the family from Texas—would have been aware of My Lai and of the Tate-LaBianca murders and of Altamont and of other abominations lurking around the corner.

"We're done," a crime scene photographer said to Maxine, emerging from the laundry room.

Maxine and I stepped into the room, which was illuminated by generator lights. Marks on the walls showed where washers and dryers had once been. The air in the gutted laundry room felt steamy, as if all the dryers were still there and turned on full blast. I wiped my brow with a tissue, which I put back into a pocket of my ratty shorts.

Arthur's corpse, outlined with tape, lay in a fetal position, its hands tied behind its back and its feet bound together with DayGlo tangerine-colored rope. A bullet, probably a .22 or something a shade larger, had entered the mastoid process, leaving a small red mark. The eyes of the corpse stared the stare of death into a void that none of us would ever see, eyeglasses hanging askew. I wanted to cover the body so that it would, at least, have some dignity.

"It goes without saying that this was an execution," I said. "Or at least it was staged to look like an execution."

Two men came into the room to put the body onto a gurney. Maxine and I stepped back to let them do their work.

"One thing puzzles me," I said.

"What's that, Fitz?"

"Why aren't there any flies in here?" I said. "Or pupae on the corpse?"

"Good questions," she said. "Let's talk about this outside. I'm dying in here."

"So am I."

Maxine and I exited the gutted laundry room. Cops huddled in groups of twos and threes, conversing one with another in low monotones. A man taller than me by two or three inches—he had to be at least six-six—approached Maxine and extended his hand, which she shook. His hair was silvery and parted on the side, and his complexion was wan, on the border of being anemic, as if he'd donated too many times to the blood bank that month. He was wearing a blue suit and a white shirt and was either a Latter-Day Saint or an FBI agent.

Maxine introduced the man to me: Agent Jon Larsen. She then introduced me to the agent.

"I didn't think you were going to give me a copy of the Book of Mormon," I said.

"Beg your pardon, Mr. Fitzpatrick?"

"Never mind," Maxine said, looking at me from the corners of her eyes, lips pressed tightly together. "Mr. Fitzpatrick sometimes has a very strange sense of humor."

"Especially at this time of the night," I said.

Larsen extended his hand, which I shook out of politeness. His hand felt cold and slimy, like a gecko one might find under a rock in a rainforest during October. After we released hands, I surreptitiously wiped my hand on the side of my shorts, making a mental note to wash my hands after I left there.

"We're asking the neighbors if they saw anything," Larsen said. "And, before I forget, I'd like to interview his wife."

"She doesn't know anything," I said.

He shuffled, looking a little nervous. "What makes you so sure?"

"I know Candy," I said. "She wasn't involved with this. There's no reason to interrogate her."

"I don't want to interrogate her, I just want to interview her—"

"I'll be there, if you do," I said, "with a lawyer and with a recording device, to boot—"

"We can't allow recording devices—"

"I know you can't, and quite frankly, I don't care," I said. "I know that when an FBI agent writes a report on a Form 302, they can put anything they damn well please into that report." I paused. "You're not going to be speaking with Candy."

His lips twisted, and now he looked like a recent, blood-drained victim of a vampire. His lower lip trembled. I knew that he wanted to say something to me, and I had an idea what it was, but his training kicked in, and Agent Larsen held his tongue.

"Frank," Maxine said, "he's just doing his job. We're not saying that Candy was involved in this."

"We'll talk later," I said, turning. I knew that my face had turned red, and not from embarrassment.

And now Mankowski and his partner, Junior, approached. Mankowski squinted, obviously perplexed by my being there.

"I thought I told you to get out of this town," he said, stopping in his tracks. He looked at Maxine and at Larsen in obvious bewilderment, bony chin thrust out. "What's he doing here? Did we authorize this? Didn't you hear what the chief said about jurisdiction?"

"He's here because I want him here," Maxine said. "And you're to leave him alone, Detective Mankowski. I know the story, and if anything happens to Mr. Fitzpatrick while he's here in

Las Vegas, you're the first person we're going to look for. Do you understand me?"

Mankowski glowered. I felt tempted to pat him on the shoulder and tell him that everything was going to be all right after he ate his sugar cookies, put his thumb into his mouth, and took a long nap.

"Do you understand me, Detective Mankowski?" Maxine said.

"Yeah, yeah, I understand you." He stared at the ground, kicked it, and his bushy mustache twitched.

"We'll discuss the absence of flies later," I said to Maxine. I nodded at Larsen. "You might try to get more iron in your diet." His eyes bulged. Then I looked at Mankowski, whose bushy mustache was still twitching, and chuckled. To his partner, I said: "I'm sure that a dermatologist can help you with that skin problem, Junior."

Then I left.

Eight

I drove back to Candy's place. It was two in the morning when I arrived. I couldn't sleep, and normally, I would have read in such circumstances, but I couldn't concentrate long enough to do so. So, I sat up in bed and watched television, an old Errol Flynn flick on Turner Classic Movies. Before the flick was over, I turned off the television set, bored.

I got up and went downstairs, walking softly on the steps so that I wouldn't awaken Candy. I started a pot of coffee, and, while the brew percolated, sat at the kitchen window and, through the jalousies, watched the rising sun, which encased the backyard in a reddish glow.

I heard Candy open her bedroom door, and her feet made soft padding sounds as she descended the stairs. She entered the kitchen, wearing her Christmas candy-striped pajamas and a pair of pink, fuzzy slippers. Her platinum-colored hair was pulled to the sides in pigtails. I greeted her and poured her a cup of coffee. She sat down at the kitchen counter, and I sat down in another high-backed chair next to hers. I told her the news.

She didn't reply. She stared out the kitchen window, at the patio furniture by the pool, which glowed reddish-orange, and then she embraced me. She didn't cry. I knew that would come later, probably later that morning. What I had just told her was what she had already suspected. Her body language showed that it was a relief to know that Arthur was no longer suffering, if he had suffered at all.

"We'll have to go to the morgue," she said.

"I'll go, Candy."

"I want to go. Did Maxine say who did it?"

"They don't know yet."

She blinked. A tear hung at the corner of her eye. "Well, at least you found him."

"I didn't want to find him like that," I said.

"Will you at least stay for the funeral, Frank? I know you hate funerals, but please, for my sake, come to the funeral."

"I'll go to the funeral and then some."

"What do you mean, Frank?"

"I owe Arthur one, as you said back on the beach. I'm going to find out who did this and something far more important."

"What could be more important?"

"*Why* they did this to Arthur," I said.

Generally, I don't drink caffeinated beverages—caffeine gives me a slight edge that I don't like—but I drank caffeinated coffee with Candy. After we finished, I told her that it was best that we probably get ready and head over to the coroner's.

🍎

Before Candy and I went to the coroner's office, I phoned Maxine and asked if she would meet us there. She agreed, and a little after nine, Candy and Maxine were standing in a hallway of the coroner's office, holding each other by the arms and talking in soft tones. Candy gasped and choked, and Maxine told her that she, Candy, was going to be all right. I walked around a corner to give them privacy, got a drink at a water fountain, and read a *Field and Stream* in a small alcove reeking of isopropyl alcohol. Maxine appeared a few minutes later and said that Candy had gone to the restroom.

"She's tough," Maxine said, sitting down next to me. I put the worn, tattered magazine aside. "Larsen and his team are going to be here in a few minutes."

"I thought I told him—"

"It won't hurt for her—"

"You never speak to a fed without the presence of a lawyer and unless you're recording the conversation," I said. I showed Maxine the tape recorder that I had brought. "You, of all people, should know that. I talked with Candy on the way down here about this, and she agreed with me. She's not going to speak with them unless I'm there, unless she has a lawyer present, and unless everything is recorded."

"They don't work that way, Fitz, and you know it."

"Oh, I know it."

"You make this sound as if you believe it's an inside job and that someone's trying to frame Candy."

"Now that you brought it up."

She pursed her lips. Her cheeks rouged slightly, just enough to show the onset of her anger. It seemed that I was upsetting quite a few people in Las Vegas.

"Do you honestly believe that, Frank?"

"Why the sudden rush by the FBI to interrogate her?" I said. "Can you answer that one for me, Max?"

"I don't think that I should have to dignify that asinine question with a response, Fitz. Keep it up and see if I'll help you with your investigation."

"I don't want to get into politics," I said. "But you yourself know the nature of the beast for which you work. Someone murdered Arthur. That's a fact. If it was an inside job, then they're going to do their best to cover it up." A beat. "And they're going to do their best to pin it on someone."

"If there is the possibility of this being an inside job, why are you talking to me, Fitz? Aren't you afraid that I'll go and help Larsen?"

"As I said, Max, I don't want to get into politics now. I consider you a good friend, and I thought that you considered me a good friend. I'd like to keep it that way."

Maxine frowned. "Then don't start moralizing and getting uppity on me, Fitz. We're all in this together. We all want to find out who killed Arthur Vogel and why."

"Good, as long as we understand that Candy isn't going to speak to the FBI or to any federal agents."

"You are impossible, Fitz." She stood and walked out of the alcove, her high heels rapidly click-clacking the tile of the hallway.

A few moments later, Candy appeared. We went to the morgue. There, an attendant removed Arthur's corpse from a freezer. Candy viewed Arthur's body and reached down and held his silent head. She then excused herself and hurried out of the room. The attendant put the corpse back into the freezer.

"What have you determined so far?" I said.

He looked over his shoulder at me. His black beard needed trimming. He looked greasy, like a diesel mechanic at a truck stop in the panhandle of Oklahoma.

"You family?" he said.

"Close enough," I said.

"From the looks of it, the death was instantaneous," he said. "We won't know until we cut into him."

"When will you have the results of the autopsy?"

"In due time," he said, and now he sounded peeved. "Any other questions?"

I noticed that there was a Daily Racing Form on one of the stainless steel tables. I walked over and looked down at the racing form. "Do you handicap?"

"Yeah, I handicap," he said, sounding very irritated.

"I used to, when I lived here in Las Vegas," I said. "Fact is, I did really well for myself."

"Oh?" Now he was definitely interested. He was looking at me. He blinked.

"Yes. I won thousands of dollars. The *Las Vegas Review-Journal* considered hiring me to write a handicapping column for the paper. I even won a couple of handicapping tournaments at the Orleans."

"Really? You were that good?"

"I was," I said, nodding.

"You don't handicap any longer?"

"I retired from it and a lot of other things," I said, turning away from him and to the racing form. "Mind if I have a look?"

"No, go ahead," he said, standing there, watching me.

So, I flipped through the racing form for the next five minutes or so, checked the types of tracks on which the races were going to occur, studied the odds, spotted a few horses that I thought would be winners, and circled them with an uncapped, red pen that was lying next to the racing form, making additional notes on the types of bets that he should place on the horses.

After I was done, I folded the racing form closed and, on its cover, wrote my cell phone number and name next to a cover photo of a jockey and his horse rounding the corner at Santa

Anita. Then I capped the red, ball-point pen and put it next to the racing form on the stainless steel table.

"Those might win you a few bucks," I said, heading toward the exit. "I wrote my contact info down on the cover. If you can, let me know the results of the autopsy as soon as you get them. I'll be more than happy to fill you in on other horses."

"Thanks," he said, now sounding very enthusiastic and no longer irritated. "Much obliged. My name's Al, by the way. Al the morgue attendant."

"My pleasure."

I stepped out of the morgue and into a hallway that reeked of antiseptics. Candy emerged from the women's restroom. I took her hand and led her out of the building. I drove us back in the Prius to Summerlin.

We sat on the sofa at her place, and she drank shot after shot of peppermint schnapps, talking about Arthur and all that he had meant to her. Then she cried, and when she cried, she cried hard, her tears falling like rain in the desert during monsoon season, figuratively speaking. I embraced her and didn't say anything. There was nothing I could say. And, while most people would have said that things were going to be all right, I wouldn't say that, couldn't say that. I didn't know if things were going to be all right.

One of the neighbors, who'd seen the local news that morning, called on the landline. The neighbor asked if there was anything that she could do. There was, I said.

"What?" the elderly woman said.

"Please come over here and keep your eye on her," I said. "I need to make a few forays."

"Beg your pardon, mister?"

"I need to leave the house for a while."

"On my way," she said.

After the woman arrived, I thanked her and walked to the Prius, which was in the driveway. It was time to get back to work.

Nine

Instead of driving through the semicircular porte-cochere at Zsa Zsa Cortez's warehouse studio, I parked in front of a used furniture store across the street. An elderly, humpbacked man, with wisps of silvery hair blown by a slight wind, swept the sidewalk in front of the store. He grunted after I stepped out of the Prius and looked in his direction. I locked the Prius with a tap on a key fob and walked across the street to the warehouse studio. When I neared the porte-cochere, I slowed my pace. Someone was arguing within the grounds, I could tell, but I couldn't make out what was being said.

I peeked around the lip of the porte-cochere and saw the tallest of Zsa Zsa Cortez's ephebes gesticulating, while Zsa Zsa—wearing an ornate, purple silk kimono—wagged his small index finger in the ephebe's face.

Zsa Zsa pressed forward, and the ephebe stepped backward, holding up his hands. Then Zsa Zsa lowered his finger, and the ephebe lowered his hands. Zsa Zsa spoke, and the ephebe seemingly listened, his head hanging down. Then the ephebe looked up and thrust out a middle finger at Zsa Zsa, who stamped his small foot.

The ephebe ran down the concrete ramp to the pock-marked parking lot and hopped onto the leather seat of his black Harley-Davidson. Zsa Zsa shouted something, but I couldn't understand what it was because of the revving and roaring of the motorcycle's engine. The ephebe donned a black motorcycle helmet. I moved away from the semicircular porte-cochere and headed across the street to the Prius. I had intended to speak with Zsa Zsa, but the ephebe's leaving intrigued me more. After I got into the Prius and turned on the quiet engine, the ephebe appeared on his Harley-Davidson at the porte-cochere, looked both directions, and then drove out onto the street, heading up it. I drove, staying behind him several car lengths, as he traveled farther and farther away from the warehouse studio.

He turned north, and I followed. In my rearview mirror, I saw a police car behind me. I grimaced. The police car, however, made a sudden U-turn and sped in the opposite direction, blue lights and red lights flashing, sirens wailing. I returned my attention to the ephebe, who continued north.

I drove by old strip malls with stores that sold junk and antiques and souvenirs and almost lost the ephebe when a light at an intersection turned red. A driver honked his car horn and raised a middle finger at me. I drove on, following the ephebe, who made a left turn, leaving the weathered business district and entering a residential neighborhood of one-story, ranch-style houses that showed the ravages of time and of a dying economy.

The motorcycle slowed down when it entered a cul-de-sac. I parked on the opposite side of the street and watched the ephebe as he killed the motorcycle's ignition and dismounted the bike. He removed his helmet and strode to the front door of a house no bigger than four hundred square feet. He knocked on the door, removed a cell phone from his back pocket, put the device up to his ear, and turned around, looking in several directions.

The front door opened, and the ephebe turned, motioning with a finger that he was on the line. The Latino closed the front door. The ephebe finished the call and placed the cell phone into his back pocket. He knocked on the door, which opened, and the Latino motioned for the ephebe to enter the house, which he did. The door closed behind him.

I kept the air conditioning running in the Prius. Across the street, a woman peeked out her front window at me, pulling back on the draperies. I waved at her, and the draperies closed. I decided it would be best if I drove around the block, in case the woman was wondering if she should call the cops. When I returned, the ephebe was mounting his black Harley-Davidson. I drove farther up the street and turned around, heading back to the cul-de-sac. The ephebe appeared at the corner of the cul-de-sac, looked in both directions, and headed back to the business district.

I followed him, and soon, the ephebe took an exit onto the 15, heading north. A few miles up the road, he took the Craig Road exit and headed west. I followed, going by the Cannery Casino, a gas station, and strip malls with many vacancies. The ephebe headed north on a street. I continued to follow him, keeping two to three cars behind. He seemed oblivious to my tailing.

He drove down Washburn, and a few minutes later, he was driving through a housing development across the street from a Latino Seventh-Day Adventist church. He drove around a corner, and when I followed, I saw him glide the black Harley-Davidson into a driveway of a one-story house. The garage door went up, and he rode the motorcycle into a garage that contained a dusty, Arctic blue dune buggy with a whip antenna. And next to the dune buggy squatted a deep freeze. I drove down the street, past a house that had a backyard converted into a *llantera*, and turned around at an intersection, heading back toward the one-story house.

I parked my car behind a corroded teal Toyota Corolla and waited a few minutes, keeping the cool, smooth-running air conditioning going as I planned on what I was going to say when I got to the front door. Then I turned off the ignition, got out of the Prius, and walked into the front yard, on flagstone steps leading to the front door. There, I rang a doorbell and stepped back a few feet, giving anyone who opened the door enough space to feel comfortable with my presence and giving me enough room to jump back in case anyone came after me or fired a gun at me.

The front door opened, and a black-haired young woman a little over five feet tall—probably in her late teens, like the ephebe—stood there, wearing an oversized white T-shirt bearing a gray-scaled image of Tupac Shakur and the lettering TUPAC SHAKUR 1971 – 1996 TUPAC LIVES FOREVER underneath the image. The shirt stopped at mid-thigh. Her darkly tanned face, legs, small hands, and small feet looked glossy because of the coconut oil that she had smeared on them. Neon purple nail polish covered her small fingernails and small toenails. Her black, silky hair hung long over her shoulders and small breasts. She was either a Latina or a dark-skinned white or perhaps a mixture of both. Or perhaps none of the above.

"Yeah?" she said. She had piercing, dark eyes, like a gypsy's.

"I'd like to speak with the young man who rides the black Harley-Davidson motorcycle."

"What for? He riding through people's yards again?"

"No, nothing like that," I said. "We have a common friend, Zsa Zsa Cortez. Would you please tell your friend that I'm here?"

"He's not my friend, he's my boyfriend," she said, and she turned her head, holding the door in place with one hand. "Hey, Jonathan, someone's at the front door to see you." She closed the front door, but not all the way, and I heard her speaking with the ephebe. The ephebe cussed, and she cussed, and then the door swung open, and he stood there, glowering at me, bare pectorals, upper arms, and shoulders desecrated with Aubrey Beardsley-like tattoos of zombies, vampires, and graveyards.

"What the hell are you doing here?" he said, his reddened eyes widening. "What do you want?" He was doing his best to disguise his Southern accent with a mock LA-tough accent.

"I'd like to ask you a few questions about Arthur Vogel."

"What kind of questions? The kind of questions you asked Zsa Zsa yesterday? You royally pissed him off, you know."

"Because of the questions I asked?"

"No, because he said you hated his art." He made a face, looking like a stone baboon, and then laughed. He leaned against the entrance to the house, and the young woman appeared behind him, telling him either to invite me inside or to close the front door so that the air conditioning wouldn't go to waste.

He opted for the former, and in less than a minute, I was sitting on a lacerated, leather sofa in a living room that reeked of stale cigarette smoke, incense, and pot.

The young woman removed her oversized Tupac Shakur T-shirt, which turned out to be her sole piece of clothing, revealing that not only were her face and hands and arms and feet and shapely legs darkly tanned, but her entire body, too. She opened a sliding patio door, stepped through it into the backyard, and closed the sliding patio door. She turned, jumped into the air off a diving board, ascended a parabolic arc, wrapped her arms around her knees, and then descended the parabolic arc into a swimming pool, making a loud splash.

Jonathan leaned back in a well-used, lacerated La-Z-Boy recliner, kicked up his bare feet, and fished through a near-empty packet of Marlboro cigarettes until he found one. He put the cigarette between his lips and lit the cigarette with a safety match that he popped with his thumb. He waved the safety match, extinguishing it, and dropped the extinguished match into a cluttered ashtray atop an end table.

"Kack's hot stuff, isn't she?" he said.

"I'd have to agree."

He laughed. He took a drag off of the cigarette and his expression became serious. "How'd you know I live here?"

"Would you like an honest answer, Jonathan?"

He nodded.

"I followed you after you had what looked like a heated argument with Zsa Zsa."

"What for?"

"Because you're smart, for one thing," I said. "Which means that you're probably very observant. Which means that you've probably observed quite a bit at Zsa Zsa's place and elsewhere."

"You think so?"

"Wouldn't you agree with me?"

"What the hell was your name again?"

"Frank Fitzpatrick," I said, my eyes watering and my nose running because of the cigarette smoke. I removed a tissue from a pocket in my ratty shorts and ran the tissue lightly over one eye, across the bridge of my nose, and then over the other eye, and then underneath my nostrils and across my philtrum.

"You a cop?"

"No, I'm not a cop." I sniffled. "You can trust me on that one."

"You do it private, right?"

"If you mean my services, yes, I work in a private capacity. I'm not a government employee."

"Good, because I hate cops." And he cussed and said what he wanted to have done to all cops, something that was anatomically impossible. He went on for a couple of minutes, spitting out his invective, with my listening patiently to it.

After he finished, I chuckled ruefully. "I don't necessarily like cops, but I don't necessarily hate them either, Jonathan."

"I hate them," he said, and he took a deep drag off the cigarette, closed his eyes, and held the smoke in his expanded lungs. He slowly exhaled, as if he were doing yogic breathing. "So, what do you want to ask me about that little man?"

"Were you at the party where Arthur Vogel got into an argument with Eliot Waxwell?"

"Maybe I was," he said, opening his eyes, and he tapped the end of the cigarette, which caused ash to descend like volcanic residue. "So what if I was? What the hell do I have to do with it?"

"Arthur Vogel was murdered," I said. "They found his body last night at an abandoned apartment complex on Harmon Avenue, between the Hard Rock and the Strip. I believe that the argument that he had with Eliot Waxwell might have had something to do with the murder."

Jonathan made a face. In the pool, his girlfriend swam smooth, even laps.

"I don't want nothing to do with murder," he said, shaking his head, staring at the far wall, upon which hung a tattered Confederate flag and several sun-faded posters of Jimi Hendrix and Jim Morrison. "I got enough trouble as it is, without something like that."

"You've obviously done time, Jonathan. Was it assault? Battery? Drugs?"

He looked at me. His upper lip quivered the way Elvis Presley's had.

"You're observant, and I'm observant," I said. "I saw you at that house. You bought something, and whatever it was that you bought, it wasn't legal. Me, I'd venture to say, by the looks of your eyes and your edginess, that it was crack. If I had wanted to get you, I would have got you then and there by calling the cops and turning you and your dealer friend in. Believe me, I have a way with cops, even if I don't like them, to get them to believe what I'm saying. So, you should know by now that I didn't turn you in to the cops. Not only that, I'm not accusing you of murder. And I'm not accusing anyone else of murder. I'm trying to discover why my friend disappeared and why he was murdered and who did it. And once I discover who did it, then I'll make accusations and only then."

"You ain't a cop, right?"

"That's right, I'm not."

"So, if I tell you something, you can't take me to jail, right?"

"That's right."

"What's in it for me?"

I removed my wallet from my front pocket and opened my wallet and held out a twenty. He took a drag off the cigarette and then snubbed out the cigarette in the ashtray, extinguishing the smoke.

"You can do better than that," he said.

I put the twenty back into the wallet and removed a fifty.

"That's better," he said, and he reached over and snatched the bill. He crumpled it and put it into a pocket of his jeans. "The more green, the more info, know what I mean?"

"Why did Arthur Vogel accuse Eliot Waxwell of fraud?"

Jonathan rocked in the chair. "Something to do with that chinky Chinaman that Zsa Zsa sucks up to, I bet. Before Waxwell and that little man got into the fight in the main room, they were standing in the back, in a little hallway, talking. I was in one of the bedrooms, smoking a joint, and I heard that little man say that he knew what Waxwell was doing and that Waxwell wasn't going to get away with it."

"What did Waxwell say?"

"Waxwell, well, he played it real cool. He kept calling that little man 'good buddy' and 'pal' and 'friend' and a bunch of other crap. That little man, though, he wasn't going to have any of it. And he said so. And when he said that he was going to the FBI or CIA, I can't remember what, but something like that, well, Waxwell told that little man he'd better keep his mouth shut, if he wanted to live to see another day."

The patio door slid open, and Kack stepped into the room. She slid the patio door shut. She had a terrycloth Pepsi-Cola towel wrapped around her elfin body, and her wet, black hair hung on her shoulders. She reeked of chlorine. She glanced at me, then looked at Jonathan and asked if she could have money for beer. He removed the fifty I'd given him and handed it to her, saying that he wanted his change back and that she was to come back home and not stop at Alexandra's house along the way. They had a party to go to that night, he said, and she was going to be ready for it, not like the last time.

She leaned over, kissed his lips, and then hurried down a hallway. The swimming pool cast rippling, diamond-like patterns on the wall.

"Bitches," he said, lighting another Marlboro cigarette. "What would we do without them?"

"Probably lead saner lives."

He guffawed and then choked for several seconds. Then he snubbed out his cigarette in the ashtray. When he caught his breath, Kack was back in the living room, wearing sunglasses, a light purple halter top, designer blue jean short shorts, and leather sandals. She told Jonathan that she'd be back in about ten minutes and then opened the front door and closed it, locking it while Jonathan stared at it.

"What happened next?" I said, turning my attention back to him.

"Oh?" He blinked, then looked at me. "Yeah, right. Well, I peeked out of the bedroom, and I saw that Waxwell was holding the little man up by his collar and grinding him against the wall. It looked kind of funny, like my old principal back in Selma, and I laughed, and Waxwell let go of the little man and looked at me and asked me what I was laughing at."

"The argument continued, right?"

"Yeah, it did. The little man broke free and said that he was going to tell. Waxwell chased him into the next room. You probably know the rest."

"I have an idea." I sniffled and got another tissue with which I wiped my eyes and nose.

"Now it's time for me to ask you a question," he said.

"What?"

"You think I'm queer, don't you?"

"Does it really matter what I think about you, Jonathan?"

"Do you think I'm queer, Frank?"

"I'd say that you engage or have engaged in homosexual behavior because you've had to," I said. "Zsa Zsa pays your bills, doesn't he, for your favors?"

Jonathan nodded. "He found me down there in Houston. He was doing some job for some humpback queer that worked in oil. I was working for that old humpback queer, taking care of his lawn and other crap like that. Zsa Zsa said he'd take me to Vegas and get me set up if I was a 'good boy.' What else was I supposed to do? I was hooked on the stuff, and I was tired of getting arrested for burglary and getting the crap beaten out of me by the pigs."

"Why does it matter what I think, Jonathan?"

His cheeks reddened, and he clenched his fists. For a moment, I thought that he was going to attack me. Then the coloring in his cheeks returned to normal, and his hands hung limp on the sides of the La-Z-Boy.

"Because you're a man who's after the truth," he said. "And, because, well, because I don't like doing what I do. If I could do something else, I'd do it. I swear I would."

"You don't have to sell yourself. There's always rehab."

"Rehab's for quitters, Frank."

"That's stale, Jonathan, and you know it."

"You know the truth. I know that you know the truth. I don't want to be a queer, and that's the truth."

"You believe that my saying that you're not means that you're not? I don't understand your logic."

"Never mind," he said, scowling. "It ain't too bad. Kack doesn't know what I do. She thinks I'm working a gig as a diesel mechanic down at one of the truck stops and dealing a little bit of pot, speed, and peyote on the side. And at least I don't get it, I give it, and when I give it to Zsa Zsa, I give it to him good, the way they gave it to me good in juvenile. That's why I'm his favorite."

I looked at the tattered Confederate flag on the wall and at the sun-faded posters and at artificial plants on mismatched pieces of furniture scattered about the room. Jonathan asked if I needed to know anything else.

"Do you know who murdered Arthur Vogel, and, if so, why?" I said.

He shook his head.

"Then I don't have any more questions, Jonathan."

"Sounds like the end of a trial," he said, and he stood, and I stood. He didn't offer his hand, and I didn't offer mine. I knew that it was time to go and turned and headed toward the door. "You tell a word of this to Zsa Zsa, and you're going to be one sorry man, Frank."

"First, I'm not going to say anything to Zsa Zsa or to anyone else about what you told me, Jonathan. Second, I don't like threats. And third, I don't take threats lightly—"

"I bet you don't—"

And before he could nail me in the back of the head with a haymaker, I leaned over and spun around, agile as a gazelle. The punch whistled by my head, failing to connect. His reddened eyes flashed, and he threw another haymaker, which I intercepted with a *tan sau* from wing chun. I threw a couple of straight blasts at him, driving him backward into the lacerated, leather sofa. He flailed his arms to ward off the blows. Then I leaned back and delivered a savate *coup de pied bas* to his shin. He yelped, and his head dropped forward. I bent my knees, and, with all of my body-weight behind the punch, threw a Western-style boxing uppercut, which connected solidly with his jaw. He grunted and staggered. I got his left arm into a catch-as-catch-can wrestling come-along hold and rammed his face one, two, three times into a wall.

Knowing that he'd had enough, I spun him around, let go of him, and stepped back. He sank to an unwashed, tessellated floor. Blood trickled thickly from his nostrils, and he had a nasty cut on his forehead. Jonathan wrapped his arms around his knees, crying and saying—no longer in a voice with a mock LA-tough accent but in a Southern gentleman's syrupy drawl—that I couldn't ever tell anyone what he had done with Zsa Zsa, not anyone, not ever.

"Have fun at your party tonight, Jonathan," I said, and I stepped backward toward the front door, keeping my eyes on him. "Next time, I won't be so merciful."

He glowered, thrusting his middle finger out at me and yelling, telling me to do things that were anatomically impossible. I opened the front door, stepped through it, closed the door, and walked down the flagstone steps leading to the sidewalk, glancing over my shoulder every other step or so to ensure that Jonathan wasn't pointing a gun at me.

The corroded teal Corolla, which Kack was driving, pulled up behind my Prius. Kack hopped out of her car, paper sack underneath one arm, containing what looked like a six-pack of beer. I noticed that graffiti covered the walls of a vacated house, probably a foreclosure, across the street.

"You look like a nice man," she said. "What's a nice man like you doing around someone like Jonathan Beard?"

"What's a nice girl like you, Kack, hanging around someone like him?"

"What else? He's got lots of money." She scowled. "He attack you?"

"He tried, but he didn't succeed."

"He attacked me once, but I fought back and threatened to cut off his set and almost did. He's terrified of me."

"Good for you." I really meant it. "You take care of yourself, Kack."

"You, too," she said, heading up the flagstone steps to the front door. "Have a good night."

Ten

I went back to Candy's place, where, according to Mrs. Cuthbert—the next-door neighbor—Candy had awoken, had drunk more peppermint schnapps, and had then fallen asleep. Candy was lying on a sofa when Mrs. Cuthbert and I checked in on her. I said that I could have my friend Lenny come over and watch Candy, but Mrs. Cuthbert insisted on staying there, saying that the Vogels had been very good neighbors to her and that she wanted to help in any way that she could. I checked the refrigerator, which needed filling, and told Mrs. Cuthbert that I was going to make a run to the grocery store.

The GPS in the Prius navigated me to a Smith's two blocks away. As I was entering the crowded parking lot, my Samsung rang. I turned off the smooth-running Prius and answered the phone, watching two elderly women walking arm in arm into the store.

"Fitz, we need to talk."

"About what, Max?"

"About last night and about the way you acted this morning." There was a long pause. "Are you still there?"

"Yes, I'm still here."

"That wasn't like you, Fitz. I've never seen you so rude before."

"I don't like Larsen," I said. "I don't trust him. Can't trust him. Won't trust him. What else is there to say, Max?"

"He's trying to help. And so am I. I think you and I need to meet tonight."

"I'm working on a case. I don't have time for meetings."

"This is about the case," she said. "I can't speak over the phone."

Then she told me that she wanted to meet on the Strip at the Bellagio at eight at the front desks. I said that I'd meet her there, then hung up, turned off the cell phone, and removed the battery. If someone was tailing me, I wasn't going to make it easy for them.

After I finished shopping, I returned to Candy's place, where she was still sleeping. Mrs. Cuthbert was in the kitchen, watching a Johnny Weissmuller Tarzan film on the small television set. I prepared us dinner—club sandwiches and two large Perrier waters—and, after dinner, I went upstairs and took a cold shower. Then I collapsed on the bed in the guest room and fell into a much needed sleep.

🍎

I awoke around six, dressed in a dark, cotton shirt and dark slacks and my Converse sneakers, and went downstairs. Candy, whose platinum-colored hair was sticking out in all directions, and Mrs. Cuthbert were sitting on the sofa, leaning toward each other and speaking softly about funeral arrangements. Candy was crying, and when Mrs. Cuthbert saw me, she said that she needed to go back home. I saw her to the front door, then went back and sat down beside Candy. The whites of her eyes were bloodshot, and she was sniffling. She blew her nose into a tissue and said that she must not have looked too good then.

I patted her shoulder. "You look okay, considering all that you're going through. Maxine wants to meet with me tonight. She says that it's about Arthur and that she can't speak over the phone."

"You're going, aren't you?"

"Of course I'm going, Candy. I owe Arthur one, remember?"

She nodded and leaned back on the sofa, supporting her head with one hand, torso twisted, legs close to her body. In any other circumstances, it could have been a pose for a photo shoot.

"I don't think you should be alone," I said. "At least not here."

"Why, Frank?"

"Because all the indicators are indicating that the situation is not safe. For starters, we have the FBI itching to get a formal statement from you. And second, I suspect that this thing might involve espionage."

"You mean that Arthur was a spy?"

"No, nothing like that. I'm convinced that Arthur was a good guy, as the parlance goes. And so does Maxine. He might have discovered something that he should never have discovered. And it might have cost him his life. And, well, that's why I don't want you here by yourself."

She sat up, leaned forward, and put a hand on my knee. "Do you think that someone's going to try to kill me?"

"Not if I can help it, Candy."

"What are we going to do, Frank?"

"We're going to pack, and then we're going to leave."

She packed, I packed, and then we got into the Prius, and I drove to Lenny's place on Spring Mountain Road. There, at his garage, I swapped the Prius for another Prius. And then I had Candy remove the battery from her cell phone, just as I had done with mine. And then I drove through residential streets off Spring Mountain Road to throw off anyone who might be tailing us.

After twenty minutes, I got onto the 15 and headed south for ten miles or so and took an exit and headed west for a little over a mile. On the side of the road stood a two-story motel. I drove to the front office, where I checked in with an alternate ID and then helped Candy to tote her bags to a room in a far corner of the first floor.

"I hate motel rooms," she said, looking at two twin-sized beds and at an overhead television set. The room smelled of must and Clorox and plastic shower curtains. "Before I got married the first time, I used to do a lot of traveling as a saleswoman for a book company. I was on the road twenty days each month. It got to where all motel rooms started to look the same."

"I hope that you brought a good book or two along," I said, looking at the television, which looked like a space alien's protruding eye. "If you didn't, watch a classic film or something worthwhile. Please avoid any so-called reality television shows."

"How long are we going to have to stay here, Frank?"

"Until I determine it's safe for you to leave, which means that you absolutely do not make any calls on your cell phone, which could expose you. Don't use or turn on a tablet, if you brought one along. And don't make any calls to my cell phone. I'll get a prepaid cell phone as soon as possible and call this room on that phone. Barring that, I'll find a public phone and call you. And if you need anything to eat, order a pizza and use cash to pay for it, of course. And be sure that it's a deliveryman before you open the door. I've got half an hour before I meet Maxine, so I'd better get going."

Candy kissed me on the cheek, and I told her to take care of herself.

Half an hour later, I was standing near the crowded check-in area at the Bellagio, Chihuly glass sculptures on the ceiling, directly above me. Slot machines whirred and giggled and whizzed and whistled and banged as their wheels spun. A wedding party sauntered by. Five bridesmaids were wearing identical maroon dresses, two of the bridesmaids carrying the ornate train of the just-married bride, who was smiling and looking at the just-married groom, a blond-haired man with horsey, white teeth who seemed to be leering, while a hyena-faced best man howled with laughter and punched the just-married groom in the arm. At a piano a few feet away, a bald, bespectacled, tuxedoed man sat hunched over. He was playing intricate jazz, his pudgy fingers gliding up and down the keyboard, as if he were making love to it, or it to him, while a tuxedoed standup bassist accompanied the pianist's heavenly arpeggios, which intermingled with the ceaseless din of the slot machines and the ceaseless chatter of tourists.

I sensed someone's staring at me, and I turned to see Maxine. She was wearing a black cocktail dress that contoured her Jayne Mansfield-like body very nicely. And she was wearing mock-diamond-encrusted stiletto high heels that tensed her naked calves and was carrying a small, black purse in one hand. She did, indeed, look like a genuine Las Vegas woman about town.

"Hey, Fitz," she said, stopping in front of me. She frowned. "Didn't anyone ever teach you how to dress for the occasion?"

"When I was a monk at Fontgombault Abbey, they not only taught me how to dress but how to pray, when to pray, when to eat, and so forth. But, since I'm no longer a monk, I pretty much do what I want."

"At least you're not wearing a horrible Bermuda shirt and those odious shorts," she said, wrinkling her nose. "We'll make do, I suppose."

"You said that you had something you wanted to tell me."

"I do, but not here," she said, wrapping her arm around mine, leading me away from the area. "Let's go get a drink first and catch up on things."

"As long as you don't consider this a date, Max."

"You can be such an ass, Fitz."

We sat at a small table illuminated by a candle in the bar in which the pianist and standup bassist played jazz. The standup bassist improvised a solo, while the pianist watched, seemingly mesmerized by the dexterity of the standup bassist's overly large hands. The bar smelled pleasantly of vanilla.

A scantily dressed cocktail waitress took our order—a gin and tonic for Maxine, a soda water with a slice of lime for me—and I told Maxine about how I had got my beachfront condo in Florida at a dirt-cheap price and how I enjoyed going to the beach each morning. She told me about her marriage to a facility manager at the Test Site, a marriage that ended when he filed for divorce and took a very high-paying job with the Department of Energy in Washington DC and took his secretary, a coed intern from a community college, along with him. Maxine asked if I missed her, and I said that if by missing her she meant that on occasion I thought about her, then, yes, I missed her.

"Now that we have the small talk out of the way, tell me what you know about what happened to Arthur," I said.

"Not here," she said. "Out front, at the water show."

I paid our bill, and Maxine and I walked hand in hand into a throng of tourists who were making their way to an exit. Outside, on the sidewalks, panhandlers sunbaked beyond brown held out Styrofoam cups, asking for spare change.

A few minutes later, Maxine and I were in front of the Bellagio waterpark. I put my arm around Maxine's waist, and she snuggled close to me. A wind blew in from the north, rustling her auburn hair and carrying its freshly shampooed scent to my nostrils.

The water show began. Jets of water leaped toward the sky, in sync with "Con Te Partiro," as performed by Andrea Bocelli and Sarah Brightman.

Maxine rested her head on my shoulder. "Cell phone off, Fitz, and battery removed?"

"Of course," I said, and I squeezed her toned waist. People watching the show oohed and ahhed as the music rose in a crescendo, and a man with a bushy, black mustache and wearing a new John Deere cap cussed when he couldn't get his camcorder to work.

"My people and Larsen's people have good reason to believe that Eliot Waxwell is behind Arthur's murder."

I remembered what Jonathan had told me. Then I lowered my hand, letting it rest upon Maxine's upper thigh. "And what's that good reason, Max?"

"We believe that he's been selling military secrets to the Chinese. Arthur somehow found out but didn't do the right thing. He made the fatal mistake of confronting Waxwell at a party. Waxwell decided to shut Arthur up for good."

The man with the camcorder threw it down onto the sidewalk and stomped on the now-broken-for-sure gadget. A woman standing next to him punched his arm, saying that he had no right to do that, it was Nadine's gift to them, where the hell did he get off doing something like that? Someone in the crowd of people watching the water show told them to shut up, and the man wearing the new John Deere cap raised his middle finger at whoever had said that, and the woman punched his arm again, telling him that he had no class, absolutely no class at all.

"Do you know who pulled the trigger?" I said.

"No," she said, and she placed her hand on my lower back, and I felt a tingle shoot up my spine. "Not yet. But we're working on it."

"What are you going to do about Waxwell?"

"Watch him for a while, according to Command, and then deal with him accordingly, if that's what it takes."

It would be either a plane crash or a car that ran off the road in the Hollywood Hills or, if worse came to worse, something like a natural gas explosion at Waxwell's mansion. I knew that Maxine's people would, indeed, do whatever it took to remedy the situation.

"You seem a little tense," she said, looking up at me.

"You know what I believe about these sorts of things," I said. "More important, you know how I feel about those sorts of things."

"That's the way it's always been done."

"I know. That's why I no longer work for your employers."

She stepped away from me, and I removed my arm from around her waist.

"You do want justice, don't you?" she said. "What difference does it make if it occurs in a courtroom or not?"

"Actually, it makes a world of difference," I said. "I believe in a thing called due process."

She chuckled ruefully, shaking her head. The water show was about over, and the man wearing the new John Deere cap was calling the woman who had punched his arm a seemingly never-to-end string of not-too-nice names. She punched his arm and said that since they had just gotten married in Las Vegas, they should go ahead and just get divorced in Las Vegas and turned around and stomped off into a crowd, heading down the Strip. The man wearing the new John Deere cap glowered at the broken camcorder and hurried off to find his soon-to-be-ex-wife. Some Latino kid—about ten years old, if that—picked up the remains of the camcorder and disappeared somewhere into the night.

"You'll never learn, Frank," Maxine said, and she looked at the artificial lake in front of the well-illuminated casino. "The world is the way it is. You can't change that. I can't change that. We just have to accept how things are."

"Perhaps," I said. "And then again, perhaps not. Now, didn't you suspect Eliot Waxwell all along?"

"Yes, we've had our suspicions, but nothing was ever confirmed. He's very sneaky, as you can well imagine. All of his cell phone calls and landline calls and e-mails are encrypted. He uses the best technology, stuff that not even the NSA has heard about. He's seen to it that his mansion in Henderson is virtually impossible to penetrate. He has the best IT people working for him, needless to say."

"So, how'd you make your discovery, Max?"

"Ancient Chinese secret," she said, popping a piece of red candy into her mouth, and I felt annoyed because of her cutesy attempt at coyness. "Point is, I can't tell you, at least not yet, if ever. But, rest assured, it was Eliot Waxwell who had Arthur Vogel put on ice. Speaking of which, when are the funeral arrangements?"

"Candy's still working on them," I said.

"If she needs any help, I can go over there."

"No worries. We have it taken care of, Max."

She shook her head. "You're not working on funeral arrangements. You're keeping her in hiding, that's what you're doing."

"Until I discover who killed Arthur Vogel, yes."

"I already told you who killed Arthur Vogel," she said, sounding exasperated. "It's Eliot Waxwell. We're going to deal with him. And we're going to see that justice is done."

"Until I have solid, rock-proof evidence, I'm not going to believe anything, Max. I'm not calling you a liar—"

"But you don't trust me, Fitz."

"Correction, Max. I don't and can't trust anyone at this time."

She sighed. The man wearing the new John Deere cap and the arm-punching woman were now walking hand in hand, laughing and kissing, as if nothing had happened. I turned around and faced the artificial lake. Overhead, the beam of a searchlight darted across the sky. The night felt warm and sticky, and I swatted at a mosquito that buzzed in my ear.

"Obviously, I can't make you leave Las Vegas," she said. "But I want you to know that I find what you just said very offensive and wish you would leave." It sounded as if she were going to cry.

I didn't respond.

She stared at the artificial lake. "We worked together for years, Fitz. If there was one person I thought who would trust me, it was you."

I didn't respond.

"You can do your own investigation, of course, but you're on your own, as far as I'm concerned."

She walked away.

"Max," I said.

She turned. Before she could say or do anything, I reached over and drew her to me. I kissed her, hard at first and then soft, feeling a pleasant tingling running from her lips to mine and then back to hers. The tip of her tongue tasted pleasantly of cinnamon, and she wrapped her arms around me, and I ran one of my hands through her thick, auburn hair. I pulled back from her, and a teenage boy on a skateboard snickered and told us to get a room. I replied that I was tempted to do just that.

"Fitz, that isn't going to change my mind."

"It's not?"

She mock-punched my arm and grinned. "You always knew my Achilles heel, didn't you?"

I released her from my embrace. "I wish we could go find a room. Right now, though, I need to check on Candy."

"Go check on her. Call me later tonight, okay? I'll be here on the Strip, playing the slots or a hand of poker."

"Will do."

I got into a taxi, driven by an Italian guy whose Bronx accent was so thick that I could barely understand him, and headed north, where I purchased a prepaid cell phone at a shop that sold cell phones and cell phone paraphernalia and curios and Hopi jewelry and beef jerky. Around the corner, under the awning of a closed cobbler's shop, I called the motel where I'd stashed Candy. The clerk at the front desk put the call through, and the receiver picked up. I identified myself, and Candy exhaled loudly.

"I was getting worried," she said. "You all right?"

"I'm fine," I said. "I'll be there in about an hour or so."

"Promise?"

"Promise. I'd better go."

I threw away the prepaid cell phone and caught another taxi and headed back to the Strip. From one of my pockets, I retrieved one of my auxiliary cell phones, into which I placed its battery, and turned the cell phone on. I tapped buttons until I reached the apps section and then opened a tracking device app. The coordinates on the screen indicated that Maxine was nearby, unaware that I had attached a small tracking device to her.

I paid the Ethiopian taxi driver, hopped out of the vehicle, and, using the app, tracked Maxine. I walked quickly, moving around slower-moving people, tourists who were busy taking pictures or jabbering about the amount of alcohol that they intended to imbibe the remainder of that evening.

The app indicated that Maxine was entering the Cosmopolitan. I stood in the shadows of the Paris. Then I turned off the cell phone, removed its battery, and pocked it and the cell phone. With a hundred or so tourists, I crossed the street to the other side of the Strip and then entered the Cosmopolitan.

Instead of walking down the main pathway in the casino, I walked among the slots, like a lost tourist searching for his lost wife. To my left appeared a bar, at the counter of which Maxine was sitting, unaware of my presence twenty feet away. I sat down at a slot machine and watched her exposed back. She swiveled one way in a chair, then the other, and smiled as she chatted into her cell phone. A bartender placed a drink—what looked like a mojito—in front of her, and she acknowledged the bartender with a wave of two fingers. A few more seconds passed, and she killed the call and picked up her drink. I stood, ready to approach her, until I saw Eliot Waxwell enter the bar and approach her from behind. He placed a hand on her lower back, and she turned, smiling, looking up into his sharp, blue eyes. He bent down to kiss her. I sat back down, watching them.

A scantily dressed cocktail waitress asked me if I wanted anything to drink, and I told her that I was fine. She moved out of my way, and I saw Maxine's kissing Eliot Waxwell. He laughed and leaned his head back, and she pushed him in the chest, laughing, too. He reminded me of a famous television evangelist in Houston because of the way that he, Waxwell, laughed. It was the laugh of a man whom no one in their right mind would possibly ever trust.

I stood, walked into the bar, and approached them.

"Fancy meeting you here," I said, placing one hand on Waxwell's back, which felt cold, and the other hand on Maxine's back, which felt hot. "You two certainly go together well."

Waxwell blinked. "We met before, buddy?"

"The other night at the party," I said.

"Right, right." He sounded very uneasy.

I removed my hands and smiled at Maxine. "And who's your lovely friend here?"

"She's—"

"I'm a business associate of Mr. Waxwell," Maxine said, cheeks flushing a slight red, lips pressed together tightly. "Not that it's any of your business. We'd like to have some privacy, if you don't mind."

I looked at Waxwell and winked. "I'm sure she's a handful, Mr. Waxwell."

"In more ways than one," Waxwell said, and he was about to laugh until Maxine gave him a mean, hard look. Now he looked like an embarrassed schoolboy caught stealing an apple from his teacher's desk.

Then he looked up at me, his blue eyes revealing his intense anger. "As she said, buddy, we want some privacy, okay? Why don't you leave before I have you thrown out of here? You remember who I am, don't you, pal?"

"No problem," I said. "I'm leaving. Have a great night."

Waxwell's two no-neck bodyguards appeared. I winked at Maxine, who glowered at me. I walked toward the exit.

I hurried among thousands of tourists flooding the streets. The beam of a searchlight probed the sky, and Latinos stood in rows on the sidewalks, handing out thin, slick magazines advertising the services of barely legal escorts. A stretch limo sped down the Strip, and bachelorettes were leaning out of the limo's side windows and ceiling window, yelling obscenities at tourists on the crowded sidewalks. A drunken man lobbed an empty Corona bottle at the stretch limo.

It was time to get back to Candy.

Eleven

Back at the motel, I parked about twenty feet away from the room, got out of the Prius, and locked the car. A tall street light in the motel parking lot had a single bulb, which was attracting moths and other insects. The air felt hot and sticky, and I was ready for another long shower after another long, exhausting day.

I headed toward the room, going through a narrow outdoor corridor. In one room, a television set blared, and in another room, I heard a man and three women talking and laughing, while another woman groaned loudly. The room where Candy and I were staying—114—had dark windows, and the air conditioning unit was on, humming loudly. It seemed as if Candy had gone to bed.

I slid a key card gently into place, and then there was the slight snapping sound of tumblers. Two green lights blinked on the door assembly, indicating that the door was unlocked.

Inside, I closed the door gently behind me and latched it shut. The room felt cool and smelled as if the air conditioner had been on for a while. It took a moment for my eyes to adjust to the dimness of the room, its sole illumination a silvery corona around the edges of the curtains, caused by the brilliant, solitary light in the motel parking lot. I saw the outline of Candy's figure on one of the twin beds, curled up in a fetal position. She seemed to be sleeping peacefully, and I smiled because of how innocent and vulnerable she appeared.

I sat down on the other bed. My feet ached, and I was feeling exhausted. I'd take a shower, and I knew that afterward, all that I would want to do would be to sleep for the next fourteen hours, and, upon waking, to go to my beach to watch volleyball players. I might be able to get in my sleep, but I certainly wouldn't be getting in my beach.

"Goodnight, Candy," I said, voice hoarse, leaning over and touching her back.

Her back felt cold, which meant that it didn't feel right, which meant that something was wrong. I fumbled with a light on a nightstand, knocked off a Gideons International Bible, and got the light turned on. I rolled Candy over. A peppermint schnapps bottle rolled off the bed and onto the floor, where the bottle thumped on the thin carpet and rolled against the Gideons International Bible, which prevented the bottle from rolling any farther.

Candy's lips had paled. I checked for a pulse. She gasped, and then I saw an empty aspirin bottle on the floor, two aspirins lying next to the cap. I shook her violently, and she groaned, and then I sat her up. Her eyes opened, and the whites and irides and pupils looked glazed. I swore under my breath and shook her again. She belched and then vomited, spewing several aspirins and what looked like the remains of cheese pizza. The stench almost caused me to vomit. She groaned, and I forced her to stand, placing one of her arms around my shoulders. She asked if she was dead.

"Not yet," I said, forcing her to walk with me. She felt twice my weight, though she was only half my weight, if that. "And as long as I can help it, you're not going to die."

"No," she said slowly, and she gasped. "No...no...no...I don't want...live...no..."

"We'll talk later about why you believed that you had to do this. For now, I've got to get you to the hospital."

"No, Frank...not worth living...not like...this..."

"It is worth living, and after I spring you from the hospital, we're going to have a nice, long talk about why this happened and about why it's never going to happen again."

I called 911 from the phone in the room and said that my friend had gone on a drinking binge. After that, I disposed of the aspirin bottle and called Lenny, letting him know what had happened. In a few moments, there came the wailing of ambulance sirens and police sirens. Candy's arm around my neck, I opened the door to the room and forced her to walk outside.

🍎

Two EMTs loaded Candy onto a gurney, which they placed into an ambulance, which sped off, lights flashing and sirens wailing. Motel residents had gathered outside, watching the goings-on. A motorcycle cop attempted to get a statement from me, but I took the Fifth, and when the cop said that he'd arrest me if I didn't cooperate, I told him to go ahead and that after the lawsuit, he might be lucky to find work as a security guard at a third-rate casino in Podunk, Missouri. He called me a name and walked back to his motorcycle.

I was getting my things out of the motel room and getting ready to check out when Mankowski and Junior appeared, parking their unmarked car behind my Prius. I placed my belongings into the trunk of the Prius and closed the trunk. Mankowski and Junior approached me. The idiot and his idiot partner grinned.

"Hey, Junior," I said, nodding at the younger man. "Any more shellac on your hair, and I bet you could do a really good Elvis impersonation on Fremont Street, provided that you could afford a glittery jumpsuit with a cape."

Junior leered and told me to shut up. Mankowski lit a Merit, its noxious smoke causing my eyes to water and my nose to run. Slowly, I took a tissue from a pocket in my slacks and wiped my nose, being careful not to make any sudden movements. Mankowski exhaled a cumulus cloud of foul-smelling cigarette smoke. I sniffled.

"I bet you're wondering why we're here," Mankowski said. His grin was wide enough for two Cheshire cats sitting side by side.

"Not really," I said. "But I imagine that you want to know what happened with Candy Vogel. As I told another would-be junior G-man earlier, some redneck motorcycle cop, I'm taking the Fifth."

"Well, we might be taking the Fifth, but you're taking us," Mankowski said, holding up a piece of paper.

Junior made a face and shook his head. I knew what the paper was: a warrant. And I had a sneaking suspicion who had issued the warrant or who had helped to get it issued.

"You're under arrest for the murder of Arthur Vogel," Junior said. "You have the right to remain silent—"

"I don't need to hear the Miranda litany," I said. "If anyone should know that, it's you two idiots. I know my rights. I'm surprised, though, that you didn't bring a SWAT team along with you. Don't you clowns generally like to batter down doors and use federally supplied armaments and tanks the way that an idiot carpenter uses a sandblaster when a piece of sandpaper would have done the trick?"

Mankowski flicked his Merit into the parking lot. "I told them that I could handle you by myself," Mankowski said, and I noticed how mean and how simian his eyes looked. "You coming in peacefully or not?"

The cigarette continued to smolder malodorously, and I felt tempted to walk over and to grind the life out of it with one of the heels of my Converses. But I knew better than to make any movement; I didn't want to give Mankowski or Junior a reason to gun me down or to shock me to death by way of Taser.

"Peacefully, of course," I said.

Junior put the cuffs on me, which snapped onto my wrists too tightly, and in the back seat of the unmarked patrol car, I looked out the window at that night's motel residents who had gathered in the parking lot to watch. A small, pot-bellied man stood there, wearing a red terrycloth robe. He was surrounded by four well-endowed women, who were taller than he was and who were obviously prostitutes. One of them was black, one was white, one was Asian, and the last, but certainly not the least in terms of endowment, was a Latina: a rainbow bordello. I wondered if he, this milquetoast, had found them in one of the slick magazines handed to people on the Strip.

Mankowski and Junior took me to the Clark County Detention Center, where other cops booked me. Mankowski and Junior watched, as if they'd scored the greatest arrest of their pathetic lives. A desk sergeant allowed me to make one phone call, which I did, to Lenny. He said that he'd get in contact with Ferguson, one of Las Vegas's top criminal lawyers, and that he'd go keep an eye on Candy. I thanked him, then hung up.

Two guards escorted me to a cell, which smelled of homeless people, urine, and cleaning solutions, in that order. One of my cellmates, a morbidly obese drunk who was sporting an Elvis Presley pompadour, said that I looked like a priest. When I replied that I had been a Benedictine monk, he offered me his bunk. I accepted but with this caveat: his giving up his

84

accommodations weren't going to earn him any extra points in heaven. He smiled and said that it didn't matter. And he said that he hoped that I had a good rest because I looked as if I needed it. I told him that I did. He embraced me like a warm, affectionate bear and bade me goodnight.

I thanked him and lay down on the bunk and closed my eyes. My temples throbbed with the onset of a migraine, which I knew that a few hours of sleep would alleviate.

When I awoke, around eight hours later, the drunk was sitting near the bed, head on his hands, which were on one upright knee. I sat up and yawned and then stood and stretched my back. The rest had done me wonders. About thirty minutes later, a bald, bloodshot-eyed Samoan jailer came to the cell, said that I was free to go, and escorted me out.

Maxine was standing in the waiting area, wearing a beige, short-sleeved shirt, beige pants, and beige-lensed sunglasses. Her auburn hair hung on her shoulders and over one eye, making her appear as if she could have been a pinup girl, circa 1960 or so. She did not smile when she saw me.

"Posted my bond?" I said to her, and the jailer who had escorted me turned around and went somewhere else, mumbling. A woman in a chair flipped through a magazine, and a toddler sitting next to her gurgled and made faces.

"Not hardly." Maxine handed me my tracking device. "Cute, Fitz. Why'd you do it?"

"You were dressed up way too fancy for me," I said, pocketing the tracking device. "I wanted to see whom you were meeting. Anyway, I thought they arrested me for the murder of Arthur Vogel."

"They made a mistake," she said. "You're no longer under arrest for murder or anything else for that matter, Fitz."

"Looks as if they're going to have a lawsuit on their hands, Max." A beat. "Just as you might. I don't take being incarcerated very lightly, you know. You've had your revenge, so, goodbye—"

"If I were you, I would take it as a friendly warning to get out of Las Vegas, Fitz. And in case you're wondering, it wasn't me who put out the warrant. I'm only a messenger."

"I'm quite content here, Max, but thanks nonetheless for delivering the thinly veiled threat. I intend to continue my private investigation into the murder of Arthur Vogel, whether you and your friends like it or not."

"They're not playing around, Fitz. I don't think you understand how serious this is."

"Oh, I understand how serious this is, Max. And are you done playing games? Am I free to go, or do you have some other trick up your sleeve?"

"You're free to go, but I'd like to have a word with you." A beat. "But not in here, Fitz."

Outside, we stood underneath a tree—a deciduous tree that looked like a fruitless mulberry, but I wasn't sure—and Maxine lit a thin cigarette, an Eve, and took a long, deep drag before exhaling. She smoked whenever she felt very upset.

"You almost blew it for us," she said. "Waxwell's suspicious now. He thinks that you're an undercover agent."

"Doesn't he suspect that you are, Max? What does he think?"

"He thinks that I work for Harrah's, that's what he thinks. And he thinks that I'm a sexually frustrated, divorced executive who's a nymphomaniac looking for a way to have her first Big O with a man. He belongs to a swingers' site, and my people created a profile that neither he nor several hundred other slime balls could ignore."

"Waxwell's your sexual surrogate?" I said, chuckling, shaking my head. "This means that he's like a doctor. Most people who go to the doctor don't have a good time. You looked, however, as if you were having a great time last night, so that must mean you had your Big O."

The corners of her lips turned down, and her cheeks turned red, meaning that the dam holding back her temper was about to burst. "I wasn't having a great time, Fitz. I was having a horrible time. He's the sleaziest man I've ever had to investigate."

"You could have fooled me, Max."

"What else do you want me to say? He's the scuzziest of the scuzziest."

"That's saying a lot, considering the people for whom you work."

"Don't start on me again, Fitz. I'm not in the mood."

"I need to go see Candy—"

"Candy's fine. She's going to make it."

"Let me guess: Larsen and your other friends are watching her, right?"

"No, your good friend Lenny is," she said, wrinkling her nose in obvious distaste. "He and his disgusting grease monkey friends won't let her out of their sight. You know some of the strangest, most distasteful people, Fitz."

"Does that include you?"

"Didn't I tell you not to do that?" she said, cheeks flushing red. "My temper's less than a thousandth of a millimeter away from blowing up."

"Perhaps you should go visit your good doctor."

"Look, Waxwell was about to tell me something about Wang and Arthur," she said. "I almost got it out of Waxwell before you showed up and ruined everything."

"Do you suspect Wang of also being involved in Arthur's murder?"

She nodded. "It's getting hot. Care to go for a ride?"

"As long as it's not my last one, Max."

"At least not this time, Fitz."

She said that she needed to check on the intranet cloud at the Test Site and that the hour-or-so-long drive up there would give us time to talk. In a few minutes, we were cruising up the 95 in a red 1966 Buick Electra 225, a classic car that she had purchased from a heavily in-debt compulsive gambler, after getting a sizeable divorce settlement from her ex-husband; Maxine loved to drive classic cars whenever she could. Even though the air conditioning was on nearly full blast, the seat of the car still felt hot from the car's having been in a parking garage that morning. The interior was shiny and well-kept, just as all of Maxine's possessions were well-kept, and smelled pleasantly of vanilla.

"Tell me about Wang and his involvement in Arthur's murder," I said.

"Wang's a conduit in this espionage game," she said. "While his shipping corporation's legitimate, his other business activities aren't. He's helping to funnel military and industrial secrets to Beijing, among other things."

The car sped up the highway and past the High Desert State Prison to our left. Heat waves shimmered on the highway. In some ways, being in that car was like being in a time machine, taking Maxine and me back further and further, years at a time, until we would arrive somewhere in the Sixties, when gasoline was cheap and people smoked unfiltered cigarettes and ate juicy hamburgers and gobbled deep-fat-soaked French fries, without worrying about lung cancer, obesity, and diabetes. I wished that we could go back in time to save Arthur, among others.

"And Wang, from what you imply, is obviously working with Waxwell," I said. "But this brings up and begs more questions."

"Like what, Fitz?"

"How did Arthur makes this discovery, for starters? And what was it, exactly, that Arthur discovered? And what is Wang's involvement, if any, in Arthur's murder?"

She didn't say anything but stared ahead at the highway through her beige-lensed sunglasses. If it had been late September, we could have ridden to the Test Site with the windows rolled down. Her auburn hair would have looked beautiful wind-whipped across her face. And the Mojave Desert is at its most beautiful that time of the year.

"We don't know exactly what it is that Arthur discovered," she said. "We just know that he discovered something and that whatever it was, Waxwell had him killed."

"And how do you know that?"

"How else? We have an informant."

"Don't tell me that it's Zsa Zsa Cortez," I said.

"Don't be ridiculous," Maxine said, sounding peeved. "I did research on him, by the way, after you brought him up at the Test Site. I don't see what anyone sees in that crap that he produces."

"Neither do I, but I suppose that I'm not a man of wealth and taste."

"What?"

"Never mind," I said. "It's an inside joke."

"Whatever, Fitz."

"By the way, who's the informant, Max?"

"I can't tell you that," she said, and for the remainder of the trip, through Indian Springs and Cactus Springs and up to Mercury, she didn't say another word.

At the Test Site, I waited in a visitors' office outside the front gates, which were guarded by Wackenhut guards wearing desert camouflage and toting 9mm pistols that dangled in low-hanging holsters. Through the front window, I watched two of the guards inspecting Maxine's 1966 Buick Electra, its trunk open. The two guards seemed to be admiring the car.

I was the sole occupant in the room and spent the time checking my text messages. Alfredo had texted me, wondering why I hadn't gone to Louie's the past few days. I texted a reply, saying that I was out of town for the time being and then texted Fiona, a good friend from Wales who was vacationing on the Riviera and who wanted to know how I was enjoying Florida.

Maxine came back to the office and said that there had been an accident in one of her areas and that she needed to check out the accident before we left. Less than half an hour later, Maxine picked me up, and we returned to Las Vegas, where I got my belongings and Candy's belongings at the motel. I told Maxine to have a good day, and she drove off in the red Buick Electra, wheels kicking up gravel and sand in the motel parking lot. Before getting into my Prius, I walked by the room where Mr. Milquetoast had been entertaining his rainbow bordello. The curtains were pulled back, revealing an empty room with two unmade twin beds. Latina housekeepers were busy at work in the room, emptying small trash receptacles and polishing furniture.

I turned and looked at the horizon, upon which Las Vegas shimmered in the August heat. I pushed a button on the fob and got into the Prius.

Twelve

I checked into the Orleans Casino, deciding that it was better if I stayed in town and at a place that I knew well. After I took a much needed shower and changed my clothes, I went to Lenny's and got another Prius, which had been checked for tracking and bugging devices, and got a Beretta 9mm and two extra magazines. I drove to MountainView Hospital on Tenaya. There, at the hospital, I checked up on Candy, who was sleeping and being watched over by Lenny's good friends, Moro and Pak, who were able to stay beyond visiting hours because of Lenny's connections. I thanked the two men.

Then I drove to Zsa Zsa Cortez's warehouse studio. When I rang the doorbell, he didn't appear, but one of his ephebes did, the one who had sneered at me and who had made it clear that he didn't like me. I asked for Zsa Zsa, and the ephebe said that Zsa Zsa wasn't there. I pressed for further information, but the ephebe told me what I could do with it and slammed the door in my face. I turned to head back to my Prius. The August sun beat down upon me, the parking lot, and anything and everything in Las Vegas.

Before I reached my car, Jonathan drove through the semicircular porte-cochere on his black Harley-Davidson motorcycle. He sped toward me, and I stepped aside before he could hit me with the bike. He spun the bike around, doing wheelies, and killed the motorcycle's engine and removed his helmet. His eyes were red and puffy, and it looked as if he hadn't slept well. A bandage covered the nasty cut on his forehead, and his nose was slightly off kilter, showing that I had broken it when I rammed his face into the wall.

"Have a good time at your party?" I said.

He spat a globule of chewing tobacco and shook his head. "Kack, the bitch, she took off with some biker from LA. She said she's tired of Las Vegas and wants to go back home."

"If that's what she wants, then good for her," I said, and I meant it, because even though I didn't know Kack, I liked her. She had spunk. But unfortunately, from the way it appeared, she had exchanged one loser for another.

"What're you doing here?"

"Looking for Zsa Zsa, what else?"

"The little queer's probably doing some sort of deal."

"Thanks for the information."

"Hey."

I turned, half-expecting that he'd have a weapon pointed at me or was charging at me for the beating that I'd given him. Instead, he had a forlorn expression on his face.

"Sometimes I get crazy," Jonathan said, "and can't control myself. You know how it is."

"No, I don't, but if you're offering an apology, don't bother, Jonathan. I'm not interested in them. I'm interested in discovering who killed my friend."

"Whatever, dude."

The front door to the warehouse opened, and Zsa Zsa appeared, dressed in an ornate, black silk kimono. He clapped his hands together, laughed, and shook his head, heading down the concrete ramp.

"Jarvis can be such a pain, pain, pain in the you know where," Zsa Zsa said, giggling, walking up to me. "When I asked who was at the door, he said it was a Jehovah's Witness. I believed him. Can you believe that? I'm glad that I looked out the window. I would have been out sooner, but that horrid elevator is on the blink again. So, what brings you to my humble abode, dearest Frank?"

"More questions," I said, and I looked at Jonathan, who leered and walked up the ramp with the exaggerated swagger of a Western gunslinger, motorcycle helmet in hand. He closed the door softly behind him.

"I'm sorry about your friend, Frank, but I've already told you what I know about Arthur," Zsa Zsa said. "What else is there to ask?"

"Actually, I was going to ask you questions about Eliot Waxwell and Wang Min."

"First, it's too hot to stay out here," he said. "And second, I really don't have anything to say about them."

"What if I told you that were your life was in danger?" I said. "Make that, grave danger. Would that make a difference, Zsa Zsa?"

"Are you threatening me, Frank?"

"I don't make threats," I said. "You're in danger, Zsa Zsa, and not because of me. I have my reasons for believing this, and, if you were smart, you'd answer my questions."

He frowned. "Oh, all right, but not here. And let me change into something more comfortable."

He went inside to change, and I went to the Prius, where I waited while the almost-silent engine idled. The air conditioning felt good and smelled sweet, and when Zsa Zsa returned, he was wearing a white, fulgent, Tommy Bahama T-shirt, khaki shorts encircled with a rope belt, and rope sandals.

I asked him where he would like to go, and he suggested a bar south of the Hard Rock Hotel and Casino. I headed east, then turned right on Paradise Road. The afternoon traffic was sparse, for which I was thankful, and at every light, we caught a green. It seemed as if something were smiling down upon us.

We arrived at One-Eyed Jack's, and I parked the Prius in the back. The bar, like the gutted old motel on Harmon Avenue, looked like a pirate's cove. Indigos and silvers bathed the interior. Spiles ran along the sides of the room, and netting and starfish and a faux parrot hung on the walls. Knotted hawsers ran along the bar, the walls, and the plank walkways that ran around and throughout One-Eyed Jack's. The counter of the bar was a deep, shiny mahogany, so well-polished that it looked as if the counter should have been in an antique store. The place had a watery-yeasty smell that most bars had.

Zsa Zsa and I took seats at the counter. A bartender wearing US Navy whites asked what we were having and then asked Zsa Zsa if had been on television, to which Zsa Zsa replied in the affirmative. I asked for a decaf coffee, which the bartender said that he would have to brew. Zsa Zsa asked the bartender if he had any sake, and when the bartender said that he did, Zsa Zsa said that he would have that. Save for a man and a woman playing pool in the far corner of the bar, Zsa Zsa and I were the sole patrons.

"Why did you say that my life was in danger?" Zsa Zsa said, his voice barely a whisper. "I don't like it when people say those sorts of things to me."

"I don't like it either," I said. "But it's the truth. You are in danger."

"But why?"

"I think you know why," I said, and I saw that his upper lip was trembling. "I've been asking questions, and every time I get answers, the one common denominator among them all is you."

"What do you mean—"

"You know what I mean, Zsa Zsa," I said, feeling irritated because I was nearing exhaustion. "Everything surrounding the murder of Arthur Vogel somehow connects back to you. I'm not sure exactly how, but you're the key, the hub of the wheel, as it were. And, if need be, I'm going to break that hub."

"Like what? Beating me up the way you did Jonathan?"

"That's not what I meant, Zsa Zsa," I said. "I don't make threats, and I don't attack people, unless attacked first. Did Jonathan tell you something different?"

"It doesn't matter what he said."

"No, it doesn't," I said. "Now, back to the matter at hand. You're hiding something, Zsa Zsa, and whatever it is, it's going to end up getting you killed."

"I'm a painter—"

"And not a very good or gifted one," I said. "I've met lots of people like you, many people who've grown up in very good homes and who were told when they were young how brilliant they were. Problem is, these people weren't brilliant, but they ended up believing that they were, never mind the evidence to the contrary. I bet your parents, no, make that your mother, told you each and every day how wonderful you were. They were wealthy, and you were their only child. Your mother was overprotective. You could do no wrong. Each and every day, she praised you for something. And you were so intelligent, according to her. A genius. She told you this every day. And you believed it.

And when she somehow got you into that art institute in San Francisco, you still believed it." I paused. "Do you believe it now?"

The bartender placed a cup of steaming decaf coffee in front of me, along with a saucer containing regular and flavored creamers. Then the bartender placed a small flagon, sitting in a small bowl of steaming water, in front of Zsa Zsa. The bartender slid a small ceramic cup on the smooth counter to Zsa Zsa. The diminutive man thanked the bartender, as I did, and he winked at us and walked over to a sink.

"Why do you say such cruel things?" Zsa Zsa said, pouring himself a shot of sake. His hands were trembling, and it looked as if he were going to cry.

"Because you're being used by Eliot Waxwell, and, from the looks of it, Wang Min," I said. "And, perhaps, someone else. Care to tell me who that might be?"

He told me to go do something to myself. Then he drank his shot of sake and poured himself another. He downed this one, too, and then poured himself another shot.

"You're drinking them too fast," I said. "You're going to get drunk—"

"That's the entire point, my dear."

I snatched the ceramic cup out of his small hand. He scowled. I placed the cup gently on the mahogany counter. The jukebox came on, and "Mother's Little Helper" by the Rolling Stones played.

"You know that Waxwell has been using you all along," I said. "He told me it was to get revenge on the upper-class snobs who think they're better than everyone else, but there has to more to it than that. He's not the type of man to spend millions of dollars on a practical joke."

Zsa Zsa sighed a long, slow exhale. He poured himself another shot of sake, but instead of downing it this time, he took a sip and then placed the ceramic cup down onto the counter.

"Eliot told me that as long as I painted what they wanted me to paint, they'd pay me big bucks and get me a gallery and host my shows," he said. "What else was I going to do? I was tired of working as an interior decorator, barely making ends meet. So, of course, I agreed to do whatever he asked me to do." He frowned, then looked down at his drink. "Why am I telling you all of these things? I feel like such a fraud."

I felt tempted to say that he felt that way because he was, indeed, a fraud, but decided against doing that. He was having a hard enough time as it was. "You're telling me these things because if you don't, you might end up buried somewhere in the desert."

His lower lip trembled, and he bit it. Tears welled up in the corners of his eyes. One of the tears trickled down his brown cheek. The bartender came over and asked if we needed anything else, and I said no, and he walked toward what looked like a stockroom.

"Here's what I believe is going on," I said. "Waxwell saw a chance, not only to play a practical joke on the cultural elite, but he also saw a way of laundering money. He found you and knew that he could use you any which way he wanted. You were hungry for money and were willing to do anything to get it. So, Waxwell promotes your so-called art around the US and the world, and he dupes gullible people into spending millions. More important, he gets Wang to start making purchases of your work at mega prices. You, of course, have no idea what's going on. You believe that you're a genius and that you're finally reaping the financial rewards that you so vastly deserve. Waxwell gives you what you think is big money, but you don't even realize that it's mere skimming. He's making much, much more off the military secrets that he's selling to Mainland China by way of Wang Min. You, you're just satisfied to purchase your ornate kimonos and your boys." I paused, letting the effect of the pause sink into his psyche. "At least they're ephebes and not catamites."

"Mother's Little Helper" faded into the background, and another Rolling Stones song began to play on the jukebox: "Gimme Shelter." Zsa Zsa poured himself another shot of sake and stared at the shiny, mahogany counter. He didn't reply.

I sipped my decaf coffee, waited about a minute, and then decided it was best that I continue.

"When people like Waxwell and Wang are done with someone, they're done with them for good, Zsa Zsa. Many people in the government are suspicious of Waxwell and Wang, and they know it. They're getting edgy right now because they're not stupid. They know that they can't launder money through the sale of your so-called artwork much longer. You might not know anything, but you're a witness. And there aren't any witnesses in Las Vegas, Zsa Zsa. They're all out somewhere in the Mojave Desert."

Zsa Zsa motioned at the bartender, indicating that he, Zsa Zsa, wanted another flagon of heated sake. The bartender said that it was coming up, and the man and the woman at the pool table kissed, and then the woman laughed and punched the man lovingly on the arm.

"What am I going to do, Frank?" Zsa Zsa said, after the bartender placed another flagon of heated sake on the bar. "What would you do if you were me?"

"I'd get out of Dodge," I said, "but first, I'd admit the truth to someone who's seeking the truth. And that someone, as you perfectly well know, is me. Is this what's been going on, Zsa Zsa?"

He was silent a moment or so while Mick Jagger sang out for someone to give him shelter, while backup singers answered that it was only a shout away.

Then Zsa Zsa nodded. "I don't know about any military secrets, but I know that I am getting way, way, way too much money for what I am doing. At first, yes, I thought it was because I was a genius. But the truth began to gnaw at me. That's why I got so angry with you when you first came to my studio. You saw right through me. You saw the ruse, and, unlike the others, you didn't fall for it. You're a very intelligent man, Frank."

"Thanks," I said, "but I'm not, really. I just pay more attention than other people."

He looked at me, blinking. "Did Waxwell kill Arthur? Or was it Wang?"

"I'm not sure yet," I said. "It could be one or the other, or it could be that both were in on it. Regardless, I'm going to do my best to see that justice is done for Arthur's sake, and, more important, for Candy's."

"Where can I go, Frank? Where's a safe place?"

"I have a friend, Lenny, who does wonders," I said. "He has lots of connections in this town. He'll arrange to get a ticket for you somewhere. Wherever it is, go. I don't care if it's Spain or Andorra or Italy or Morocco. Wherever it is, you go, and you stay with his connections there. After all this stuff blows over, you can probably come back to the United States."

"When I come back—"

"*Probably* come back," I said. "I'm not sure how the US government is going to look at this. The feds might consider you part of the problem. And, whatever you do, don't speak to any cops or feds without your lawyer being present, and don't accept any offer from a cop or a fed without consulting with your lawyer." I frowned. "Cops and feds are very good at lying."

"Can you tell if a cop or fed is lying, Frank?"

"Of course I can."

"How?" he said.

"It's easy." I finished my decaf coffee. "Their lips are moving."

We were silent a few moments. The bartender was on the floor, sweeping it.

"I don't want to die, Frank." Zsa Zsa grabbed my forearm; his small, frail-looking hands had a death grip on me. "Please, don't let them—"

I pried my forearm from the tight grip of his small hands. "As soon as we're done here, I'm going to call Lenny. And, after that, we'll go back to your place, where you'll get your passport and a few of your things. If your ephebes ask what's going on, you tell them that you're making an emergency trip to Seattle. If they insist on going, tell them that they can't. Then I'm going to take you to a place where we're going to wait until Lenny or one of his friends comes to get you. Meanwhile, I'm going to continue my investigation. You'll soon be out of the country and in a safe place, Zsa Zsa."

"What about my boys, Frank? Are they going to be safe?"

"Don't worry about them. I'll take care of them."

"What about setting the alarm at my studio?"

"It won't do you or anyone else any good," I said. "So, why bother asking?"

Thirteen

I drove us back to Zsa Zsa's warehouse studio, where he gathered a few of his things into a small, expensive, leather suitcase. Jarvis, the ephebe who disliked me intensely, cornered Zsa Zsa and demanded to know where Zsa Zsa was going. Zsa Zsa, following the script, said that he had to make an emergency trip to Seattle; one of his relatives was in an emergency room. Jonathan was leaning back on the red, Victorian sofa, bare feet kicked up on a table. He was smoking a clove cigarette and watching a football show on ESPN. He didn't look at me or say anything to me. The other ephebe lay curled up on the floor in front of the television set, snoring softly.

Lenny had told me to call his friend Lorraine. I called Lorraine on a pay phone at a small casino on Fremont Street. I told her what needed to be done, and she said that she would see to it right away. Half an hour later, she drove a refurbished, white Lincoln Continental into the parking lot of the Spearmint Rhino, a strip club where Zsa Zsa and I were waiting. I told Zsa Zsa that Lorraine was his ride to safety. He leaned over in the Prius to embrace me, but I held up my hands.

"No need for that," I said. "You'd better get going."

He looked hurt. "Please, take care of yourself, Frank."

"I will. And you too, Zsa Zsa."

He opened the car door, suitcase in hand.

"Zsa Zsa?"

He looked back at me.

"How much money do you have on you?"

"Five thousand," he said. "Why?"

"Give it to me."

"Are you insane?" he said, and now he looked as if he had returned to his old, petulant self. "I might need those funds to survive—"

"Lenny and his friends will make sure that you're fine," I said. "Just give me the money. I'm going to use it to protect your boys."

He opened a small, pink, Prada purse that was swung over his shoulder and handed me a wad of bills, which I folded and placed into my shirt pocket.

"Thank you," he said, and he turned and walked to the Lincoln Continental.

Lorraine waved at me. I waved at her, and the Lincoln Continental sped out onto the street, heading north. I drove the Prius onto the street and headed south, taking a long, meandering drive through Las Vegas, ensuring that I wasn't being tailed.

When I was ensured of that, I drove to Zsa Zsa's warehouse studio, driving through the semicircular porte-cochere and parking next to Jonathan's black Harley-Davidson. I let myself inside with a key on a set that Zsa Zsa had given to me and closed and locked the heavy door behind me. The Beretta 9mm felt cold and impersonal at the small of my back. I pushed the button for the elevator and then remembered that the elevator wasn't working. I walked up two flights of stairs in a stairwell adjacent to the elevator shaft.

The door that opened to the living room was locked; from the other side, I heard the sound of a sports program but no movement.

The hairs on the back of my neck stood up. I moved away from the door and waited a few moments, listening for any sounds of movement that might come from the other side of the wall. There were none. I removed the Beretta 9mm from the small of my back and chambered a round. Gun in one hand, I unlocked the door softly, opened it, and stepped back, in case anyone fired a shot or leaped at me.

No one came rushing out, and no one fired a shot. I peeked around the door, then entered the room.

A coppery stench had filled the room. Jonathan's corpse was sitting up on the red, Victorian sofa, which was blood-soaked. His throat had been slit from ear to ear, his raw, cut-open esophagus exposed obscenely. The head of the corpse was leaning back on an ornate knob on the sofa's dark frame. Several puncture wounds dotted the corpse's chest, and its bloodied forearms and arms showed defensive wounds, indicating that Jonathan had put up a good fight. Strangely, the expression on the corpse's face was one of peace, where, when Jonathan had been alive, his expression had been one of deep anger and deep pain.

The ephebe who had been sleeping in front of the television set was still there. Rather, his corpse was. Someone had fired what appeared to be a small-caliber slug into the ephebe's temple. From the looks of it, the ephebe hadn't awakened, which probably meant that he had been either too drunk or too stoned to wake up.

I left the gory room and its overturned furniture and walked into a kitchen, where I found the corpse of Jarvis, the ephebe who had disliked me so intensely, lying face down on a black-and-white-tiled floor. In the palm of an outstretched hand lay his cell phone; he'd obviously tried to make a call, probably to 911, before someone shot him several times in the back.

Then I heard what sounded like something falling in Zsa Zsa's spacious studio down the hallway. I crept along its sides, holding the Beretta semiautomatic with both hands, ready to squeeze off rounds.

When I neared the door to Zsa Zsa's studio, I heard two men speaking in Cantonese. One of them was speaking loudly, obviously scolding the other. Then there was silence, followed by the sound of liquids splashing onto the studio's hardwood floor. Almost instantaneously, the hallway reeked of paint thinner. It didn't take a genius to know that the two men intended to torch down the place.

I jumped back, crouching behind an ornate, Meiji-era bookcase filled with several dusty tomes. The door to the studio opened, and out stepped a man dressed sartorially in a Brooks Brother suit. He had a scar resembling the east coast of South America, a scar that ran from the corner of his left eye to the corner of his small mouth. I recognized him as one of the men who had been speaking with Wang Min at the party. The man's hands appeared bloodied and bruised, probably from the brutal fight that he had had with Jonathan.

The man turned to speak to his partner, who was following close behind and who was about to flick an ormolu lighter. I

stepped out from behind the bookshelf and slapped the scarred-
face man in the back of the head with the butt of the Beretta.
His partner leaped back, startled like some kid who'd just been
caught sneaking into the afternoon matinee by a theater manager. I had the Beretta down at my side, trained on the partner's
stomach. Like the scarred-faced man, the partner was wearing a
Brooks Brothers suit.

He raised his hands slowly, and I told him to drop to his knees
quickly. I sidestepped him and stood behind him. Then I struck
him in the back of the head with the butt of the Beretta, knock-
ing him out. I kicked the ormolu lighter aside. I gathered sheets
from one of the guest bedrooms and bound the hands and feet
of the two unconscious men and then wiped any surface that
might have my fingerprints.

After that, I went back into the kitchen, where I scooped up Jarvis's
iPhone from the hand of his corpse. Using the iPhone, I took several
pictures of the corpses and of the two bound, unconscious men.

And, after that, I closed the door to Zsa Zsa's warehouse studio
behind me. I drove out of the semicircular porte-cochere and
headed up the street. I parked in front of a swimwear boutique, its
windows covered with wrought-iron bars and its walls covered with
highly calligraphic gang graffiti. I dialed 911, using the iPhone.

"Is this an emergency?" the 911 operator said, sounding wea-
ried but doing her best to sound concerned.

"If you consider murder an emergency, then yes, it is," I said,
doing my best to disguise my voice. I gave the address to Zsa Zsa's
warehouse studio, told her what the cops would find there, killed
the call, and then removed the battery from Jarvis's cell phone.
Then I drove to Binion's.

After a quick dinner at Binion's, I walked out under the
canopy that covered Fremont Street and called Lenny. I told him
that I needed to exchange the golf cart, which was code meaning
that I might be in deep trouble and that I would be heading over
to his place in a few moments. I was certain that security cameras
had caught the Prius on tape.

Somewhere in the distance, sirens wailed. Three police he-
licopters flew overhead to the north. The sky to the west had
crimsoned, and it still felt very hot and humid. I went back into
Binion's, got my parking validated, and then left old Las Vegas.

Fourteen

At Lenny's, I exchanged the Prius for a Volkswagen Jetta and then drove to MountainView Hospital. The sky had deep-blued and had hints of light purple. I quickly uploaded the pictures that I had taken into seventeen encrypted repositories. Before I went to Candy's room, I spoke with her doctor, who was making his rounds on the floor where she was staying.

After I finished speaking with the doctor, I entered Candy's room. Moro and Pak were no longer there, but Siegfried and Hans, identical twin bikers from Hamburg, were. They stepped out of the room to give Candy and me privacy, and Candy smiled when she saw me, reaching out to take my hand. I felt a catch at the back of my throat. The room smelled of cleaners and other hospital smells that I didn't like.

"What got into you, Candy?" I said. "Why did you do it?"

"I'm sorry, Frank." A tear appeared in one eye, and she removed her hand from mine and took a tissue from a box near her bed to wipe away the tear. She was wearing a Seattle Mariners baseball cap, into which she had stuffed her platinum-colored hair. "I didn't mean to put you through this. It was just the strain—learning that Arthur had been murdered and then feeling as if I were going to have to live my life always on the run. So, I went to the CVS down the street." A beat. "Take it from there."

I sat down on the bed. My feet and my legs felt tired, and I was hungry and ready for a good night's sleep. The day—make that my entire stay thus far—had been exhausting. I yawned and covered my mouth.

"A psychiatrist came by," she said.

"And?"

"I said that I didn't feel like talking and that I was okay and that I had had way too much to drink. She said that she would come by later. She reminds me of my kindergarten teacher, who was a mean old biddy of a spinster." She blinked. "Lenny told me what you did for me. Thank you."

"Did you say anything else to the psychiatrist, Candy?"

"Nothing."

"Good," I said.

"She kept asking me if I felt safe at home and if I had any guns in my house. It was like she was playing Twenty Questions."

"She was," I said, "but keep in mind that the questions aren't to help you, they're to mine information about you. Whatever you said, you can rest assured that it's going to end up in a government database, if it's not there already."

"Speaking of the government, Larsen came by. Moro and Pak chased him off. Before he left, he said that I'd better reconsider talking to them."

"You remember what we talked about, right?"

She nodded.

"Good." I paused. "I spoke with the doctor, and he said that you can leave in the morning. I'll come by first thing to get you." I paused. "Things are getting hairy out there."

"In what way, Frank?"

"We'll talk about that later, Candy." I paused. "You get some rest. See you in the morning."

I thanked Siegfried and Hans and drove to the Orleans Casino, where I took an elevator up to my room. There, I took a long, cold shower, dressed in a Bermuda shirt and baggy shorts, and then turned on the television set. It was a little after ten.

I changed the channel from Investigation Discovery to the local NBC affiliate. A reporter—a blond-haired kid barely out of college, from the looks of it, with a haircut that looked as if it could have been hit by the winds and debris from a megaton blast and still have each strand of hair stay in place—stood in front of an inferno, microphone in hand. Immediately, I recognized the place as Zsa Zsa's warehouse studio.

The blaze, according to the reporter, had started sometime after six that evening. No one knew the whereabouts of Enrique Cortez, the world famous artist who owned the studio. The police, said the reporter, were looking for a vehicle of interest. I held my breath for a split second. On the screen appeared a blurry image of the Prius that I had been driving. According to the reporter, it was suspected that one, if not more, people were in the warehouse. Their conditions were not known at this time. The reporter didn't mention any suspects or physical descriptions of any suspects.

As he continued to speak, the camera panned to the left, showing the warehouse, which was engulfed in flames. Firefighters fought feverishly to put out the fire. Cops stood on the scene, in groups of twos and threes, watching the blaze. An ambulance stood ready.

I turned off the television set. I was tired. I was tired of watching and listening to the damn thing. I was tired of my stay in Las Vegas. I was tired of being tired.

I turned off the lights. At first, I thought it was going to take me a long time to fall to sleep because of how active my mind was. But in less than ten minutes, I was out.

&

I awoke around six. Sunrays made their way through chinks in the dark-colored draperies, striking the door in golden shafts. After taking a quick shower and dressing, I went downstairs and partook of a buffet breakfast in one of the restaurants, which smelled pleasantly of warm pastries, breads, eggs, bacon, coffee, and other breakfast items. Agile waitresses dressed in purple, green, and gold outfits poured coffee, orange juice, and other breakfast drinks. Most of the patrons in the restaurant were elderly tourists who made small talk about the previous day's bus ride to the Hoover Dam. Had I been in the restaurant under different circumstances, I would have enjoyed listening to their innocent chatter.

At a corner table, I read an abandoned *Las Vegas Review-Journal*. On the cover was a photograph of the charred remains of Zsa Zsa Cortez's warehouse studio. The police, according to the article, were still seeking a Prius and had found three bodies in the debris. A grainy photograph of the Prius stood above the main text of the article, and above the grainy photograph appeared a color photograph of Zsa Zsa's warehouse studio going up in flames. A side bar about Zsa Zsa presented a schematic bio of him, along with quotes from celebrities who admired his work.

A bone-thin waitress asked me if I needed any more decaf coffee. I told her no, read a news article about a civil war brewing in Oman, and then read the funnies.

After I finished, I went to the parking garage and got into the Jetta. I removed Waxwell's business card from my wallet. His business address was on Howard Hughes Parkway. I knew the area and wouldn't need to use the GPS to get there.

I arrived at a business park about twenty minutes later and parked the Jetta in a visitor slot in front of the Waxwell International building. The morning was already hot and humid, and the air smelled fetid, like a greenhouse. Sprinklers on the lush lawns surrounding the building shot water in arcs that formed knee-level-high rainbows. A harsh wind blew, and palm trees, which lined the concrete pathway leading to the front door, swayed. The iridescent windows of the building reflected that morning's sunlight, nearly blinding me. The wind blew harder, and I hurried up the concrete pathway and into the lobby of the building.

A bored-looking security guard, a man with rheumy, blue eyes and a white mustache, peered up from his desk at me. Two armed security guards stood behind him, their arms crossed. The bored-looking guard asked what I wanted. I said that I was there to see Eliot Waxwell and gave the security guard my name. He snorted, picked up a telephone receiver, and pushed an illuminated button on a console. He spoke in muted tones, covering the receiver with a large, liver-spotted hand and keeping his rheumy eyes on me. After a few seconds of silence, his eyes widened, and he put the telephone receiver back into its cradle.

"Sign in here, please," the guard said, pushing a ledger toward me on a glass counter. "Didn't mean to sound so rude, but we get crazies coming up here all of the time to see Mr. Waxwell. We have to be careful, you know." He held up a semiautomatic pistol. "And I'll need to see a photo ID, please."

"No problem," I said, signing the ledger and entering the time of my visit and wishing that he would put away the pistol, which he did after I slid the ledger back to him and showed him my photo ID.

"Any elevator will take you to the twentieth floor. That's where Mr. Waxwell has his personal suite and that's where he said that you're to go."

"Thank you."

"You're welcome. Have a great day, sir."

I arrived on the twentieth floor a minute or so later, after a smooth ride on an elevator. A secretary was sitting behind a large, circular, basalt desk in a dimly lit reception area. Prokofiev's *Peter and the Wolf* played softly in the background.

The secretary stood. She reminded me of Marie LeBeau, the vulpine manager at the Jacobs Gallery in the Miracle Mile Shops. Unlike Marie LeBeau, however, this woman had black hair, and her fingernails looked like sharpened bits of silicate.

"Mr. Waxwell will see you in a few moments, Mr. Fitzpatrick," she said, motioning with her left hand for me to have a seat on a low, black sofa that ran along the back wall of the reception area. "Would you care for something to drink? Coffee, tea, or water?"

"No, thank you," I said, taking a seat. I studied her vulpine features, especially the sharp tip of her nose and tapped a finger on my knee. "You remind me of someone."

"Oh, really?"

"You do," I said. "Do you happen to have a sister?"

"I don't discuss family," she said. "Why do you ask?"

"No particular reason. As I said, you remind me of someone."

"Oh."

She excused herself and sat down at her workstation. From my vantage point, I saw that she was working on an Excel spreadsheet. She adjusted calculations in columns and then changed the tab on the spreadsheet and generated several pie charts on the new tab. Her fingers moved dexterously, her silicate nails tapping keys at least one hundred words a minute. To say that I was impressed would be an understatement.

"Frank," I heard Eliot Waxwell say, and I turned, seeing him walking toward me, hand extended, Southern-boy grin on his face, making it look as if he was happy to see me. He was wearing a tailor-made suit, perhaps something purchased in London, Paris, or Stockholm. I stood and shook his hand. "What can I do for you today, Frank?"

"It's a private, urgent matter," I said. "I think it's best if we talk about this in your suite."

"Of course." He turned and led the way into his suite, closing the door behind us.

The expression on his face changed from Southern-boy grin to outright rage. He thrust his finger at me, his body trembling.

"I am tired of you," he said, and his spittle almost landed on my shirt. I took a step back, and he took a step forward. "I told you, I don't know about your friend. And as for the casino, what I do is none of your business. And I don't know how you found me there, pal, but believe me, you aren't going to do anything like that ever again. Got me?"

"I'm not here about Arthur Vogel," I said, watching him, wondering if he would attack. He seemed to become less tense, and he took a step back, giving us both more space. "This is about Zsa Zsa Cortez. You are aware that his warehouse studio burned down, aren't you?"

"Hell, yeah, I know," Waxwell said, and he went to a small bar and picked up what looked like a scotch and soda. He downed the contents of the heavy tumbler, and I could hear the ice clicking against his teeth, a somewhat pleasant sound. He placed the tumbler down next to an empty bottle. "You think I made my billions not knowing what's going on around me?"

"They found bodies in the debris," I said.

"So?"

"Do you know who they were?"

He glowered. "What do you think?" And he called me a few names and went to a window, which, inside, was heavily shaded but not iridescent.

"You seem very tense, Mr. Waxwell."

"Wouldn't you be in a situation like this? I put millions upon millions of dollars into that little queer, and now everything is lost. What's Wang going to say when no one there's to paint his mural in Macao?"

"I know that you detest Zsa Zsa Cortez and his work," I said, "but why not find another third-rate abstract expressionist? There are plenty of them out there. Just go to the fine arts department of any state university. More than likely, you can pull another one of your practical jokes on the public, and more than likely no one will get it."

"No, they probably won't get it." And then he told me to do something anatomically impossible.

"This isn't about the burning down of the warehouse studio, Mr. Waxwell. And this isn't about Zsa Zsa Cortez. This is about something else, and this something else is eating you from the inside out."

We didn't speak for a few moments. He opened a sandalwood box on his uncluttered desk and removed what looked like a Gitane cigarette, which he lit with a small, globular lighter next to the box. The smoke whisked upward into a ventilation shaft, drawn there by a fan, for which I and my nostrils were thankful.

"One thing bothers me," I said.

"What?" I could tell that he was about to explode because of the way he was clinching his jaw muscles and the way in which the tendons in his neck stood out.

"Why did you agree to see me?"

He bit the corner of his mouth, and I knew that he was holding back choice words. I walked to a window in the penthouse suite that overlooked Howard Hughes Parkway. From that vantage point, I got a good view of the Strip and the numerous casinos on it. Tourists would be checking out that morning, and a new herd of them would be arriving in this ersatz paradise.

"You're here," he said, "because I suspect something, Frank."

"What do you suspect, Eliot?"

"You know who the victims are, don't you?" he said. I turned. He was looking at me, no longer looking like that world-famous huckster from Houston but like a wounded dog. "I know what a man like you is all about. You wouldn't come up here if you didn't know something. You're baiting me. You're trying to see what it is I'm up to. It's like we're playing chess. I might have more pieces than you, but you have some sort of strategic advantage that I don't have. Chess, hell, this is more like a puzzle that you're solving on your own. Others can't see how to complete it, but you're beginning to. And you have a few pieces of that puzzle in place, and you came up here to confirm that and to see what else you could do to get a few more pieces put in place. Well, I'm going to tell you this, friend, this is a whole lot deeper than that." He spat vituperations, refusing to look at me, his face turning red. "A whole lot deeper, deeper than the well in my grandma's back yard down there in the Florida panhandle, that's for sure."

"I'm familiar with two of the victims and somewhat acquainted with one," I said, deciding it was better to play things straight
instead of indirectly, at least for now. "They were Zsa Zsa's boy-
friends. As for the men who seemingly killed these ephebes, I saw
one of the men at that party."

"You were at Zsa Zsa's place before the building burned down,
weren't you?"

"Yes, I was."

He snorted. "You got balls, Frank. Whoever went there, they
went there for Zsa Zsa. I know that."

"I don't believe that it was for Zsa Zsa," I said. "I believe this
had to do with what Zsa Zsa was doing. My friend, Arthur Vogel,
was interested in what Zsa Zsa was doing but not in Zsa Zsa, *per
se*. From what I know about Arthur, he would have found Zsa Zsa
not only irritating but highly vacuous, just as I do. The murderers went there to destroy the warehouse, which was their primary
concern. The murders were only ancillary, necessary so that there
wouldn't be any witnesses."

"You know that, then you probably know where Zsa Zsa is," he
said, and he snubbed out the Gitane in a glass ashtray that looked
like a glob of red lava. "Where is that little queer?"

"I don't know," I said. "And even if I did, I wouldn't tell you."

He sighed. "They're on to us, aren't they?"

"Whom do you mean by 'us'?" I said.

Now he looked at me, and instead of looking like a wounded
dog, he looked like a rabid one. "Who do you think, Frank? The
feds. They know what's been going on, don't they?"

"If not, they soon will be," I said. "I suspect what you and
Wang have been doing, though I can't be sure. And, before I
came up here, I wondered if I should speak with you. I didn't
know if I would come out of here alive." A beat. "I'm still not
sure."

"Well, you don't need to worry that little head of yours,
Frank," he said, and he stood and walked around the desk, hands
at his sides, doing his best to appear like a competent business-
man: calm, cool, and collected, in that order. "So, what do the
feds know?"

"Probably a little bit more than me," I said. "They believe that
you've been selling military and industrial secrets to the Chinese.

And they believe that you and Wang Min are colluding. And I believe that you are doing this through Zsa Zsa's paintings. They aren't mere abstractions; they're codes of some sort. From the looks of it, they're passwords to cloud Internet sites or to intranet sites or both."

His eyes widened, as if I had shocked him from this universe into the next, and then his expression changed from one of shock to one of mirth to one of contempt. He laughed and shook his head and went back to his desk, where he sat down.

I watched him for a couple of minutes. He was laughing so hard that his face turned a dark red, and tears welled up in his eyes, which he wiped with a monogrammed, silk handkerchief that he removed from a pocket in his suit jacket.

After another minute or so passed, he stopped laughing, coughed, wiped his mouth with the silk handkerchief and folded it, placing it back into the pocket in his suit jacket after he had finished the folding.

"I can't believe you said that," he said. "And I thought for a moment that you were on to me."

I didn't say anything. I didn't know if he was bluffing. After all, he hadn't made his billions by allowing others to see his intentions. He would have a made a great championship-level poker player.

He stood, pointing at the door. "You get out of here, Frank." He was smiling like a homeless schizophrenic, which I found unpleasant. "You get out of here now and never come back, understand?"

I turned and, without saying a word, headed toward his office door. Waxwell slammed the door behind me. In the dimly lit reception area stood the two gorilla bodyguards, no necks, arms crossed, both bodyguards glowering at me. The secretary looked up from her Excel spreadsheet, in the nervous way that a ground-hog pops its head out of its hole, then looked down at her screen. One of the bodyguards extended his arms into a stretch, and I told him that Walgreens sold a very good underarm deodorant, if he was ever in the market for it. He started for me, but his gorilla no-neck partner, who was laughing, held him back.

Outside, in the parking lot, I put the battery into my cell phone, powered it on, and listened to my messages. Marnie, a friend in Seattle, had called me, and after listening to her message, I listened to a message from Al the morgue attendant, for whom I'd handicapped. The message was marked urgent. He sounded breathless in his message, and he told me that I had to call him back on his private cell phone immediately, which I did.

"Yeah?" he said, after picking up on the second ring.

"This is Frank Fitzpatrick. You asked me to call."

"Right, right, hang on." I heard the banging of metal, his cussing under his breath, and the opening of a door. A woman with a deep voice spoke in the background, and Al the morgue attendant said that yeah, yeah, he would be on it right away, and couldn't she see that he was dealing with urgent morgue business, couldn't she see that?

It sounded as if he had entered another room, and then he spoke.

"They never give you a moment's rest around here," he said. "You'd think that dealing with all of these dead bodies would give a guy that right, right?"

"What's this about?" I said. "You said it was urgent."

"Oh, yeah, right, right." He cleared his throat. "I followed your advice and scored big time to the tune of two grand. Two grand! Isn't that crazy? God, I hadn't had a win in a long, long time. Everyone was asking me how in the hell I did it. Of course, I wasn't going to tell them about you. Hell, why would I? That would be cutting my own throat. You have a gift, a real gift—"

"Is this all you called me about?" I said. "What about the autopsy?"

"Oh, yeah, right," he said. He paused, then spoke. "Look, let's talk about this in person. Can you get here right away?"

"Yes, I can."

"Okay, good. Look, I got a racing form, too, and was wondering if we could go over it."

"No problem," I said. "I can be there in twenty minutes. Now where, exactly, are we going to meet?"

He was wearing green scrubs and smoking a cigarette in a smokers' area. And even though he was dressed in green scrubs, I still envisioned his working at a truck stop somewhere in the American heartland, sweating and huffing and puffing over a diesel engine. He smiled when he saw me approach and thrust out his hand, which I decided to shake out of tact.

"What about Arthur Vogel?" I said, removing my hand from his cold, rigor-mortis-like grip and stepping back because he smelled of the dead. "What did you discover?"

"He'd been dead four to five days before they found him at that abandoned motel," he said. "He had marks on him like he'd been in a freezer. He was killed with a round from a .32. We sent that to the police, of course, for examination and evidence."

"It doesn't sound as if he suffered."

"Not from the looks of it," Al the morgue attendant said. "That entrance wound was the only wound we could find. It was definitely an execution. Your friend was dead before he hit the ground." The morgue attendant frowned, then dropped his smoldering cigarette into a butt receptacle and wiped his nicotine-stained fingers on his smock. "There was one strange thing, however."

"What's that?"

"We discovered radioactive particles on him," he said. "Since he worked at the Nevada Test Site, we decided to go ahead and do a quick check. There were trace amounts, but it meant that he had been in a radioactive area."

"Do you know the element?"

"Uranium, but don't ask me about the isotope, because I don't know," he said. "You want that answer, you'll have to talk to the coroner or get ahold of the report."

"Which they won't give to me, at least not at this time."

"No, they won't." He removed a racing form from the small of his back and held the form and red pen out to me. "You don't mind, do you?"

"Perhaps you should learn how to do this yourself someday," I said, taking the form and the pen. I sat down on a bench, opened the form, and uncapped the pen. "I can't keep doing your handicapping for you."

He sat down next to me. "What if I split the winnings with you? We'll make it sixty-five, thirty-five. Since it's my money, I get the bigger share. What do you think?"

"Not interested," I said, and I started to handicap and gave him a few pointers on how to pick the winners. I told him, of course, that nothing was surefire and that he was probably wiser to go to a financial adviser and to invest his money, instead of playing the horses. I could tell that he wasn't really listening, though, and so went on with the tutorial and chose what I considered to be winners.

After I was done, he profusely thanked me and hurried off.

Then I went back to the Jetta. It was time to pick up Candy.

Fifteen

We checked on the house in Summerlin and then headed over to the Orleans, where we went up to my room. I called room service and ordered two pots of coffee, one regular, one decaf. I opened the dark draperies, and August sunlight flooded the room. Down on the street, at an intersection, a cornrow-haired man had a nickel-plated-looking boombox to his head. He danced in circles, his loose, black pants hanging at mid-thigh, revealing plaid boxers. I turned away from the window and sat down in one of the chairs beside a table.

"Discover anything?" Candy said.

"Suffice to say, nasty things are gestating at this time. I met with Eliot Waxwell this morning, by the way."

"Why?"

"Because I thought that I was on to something. From the evidence, it appeared as if Eliot Waxwell and Wang Min were in cahoots, shipping off military and industrial trade secrets to China. After my meeting with Waxwell, though, I knew that I was way off."

"So, what, exactly, did you do?" she said.

"I confronted him with what I knew, playing my hand to see how he would react."

"And how did the sleaze ball react?"

"He laughed, as if he were insane," I said. Room service arrived, and I tipped the server and closed the door behind me before putting the two coffee pots onto a table. I poured coffee for Candy, then for me. I sat back down. "At first I thought he was bluffing. But he wasn't. And he wasn't insane."

"What was he, then?"

"Relieved." I put creamers into my decaf coffee, stirred it, and then sipped it. It was fresh and scorching hot, the way I liked it. "He was genuinely relieved that I didn't know a thing."

Candy sighed. "Arthur's dead, Frank. You didn't promise to find him, but find him you did. You've done your part. I think that you should go back to Florida."

"I think we've had this discussion before, Candy," I said. "I am not going back to Florida. I'm going to solve this case. I've been harassed by inept cops, had to play psychodrama with a neurotic third-rate painter, and had to spend the night in a cell in what is euphemistically called the Clark County Detention Center, but which, in the old days, was properly called a jail." I sipped my decaf coffee. "I've gone through too much to give up now."

We made small talk after that, and around eleven, I told her that I was going to leave and that I wanted her to come along with me.

"I thought you preferred to work alone," she said.

"I do, Candy, but I want you around me as much as possible from here on out."

"Afraid that I'm going to try to do it again?"

"No, I'm not. But I don't think I could face myself if I left you vulnerable and someone did something to you."

"What are we going to do, then?" she said.

"We're going to do a little spying, that's what we're going to do."

We left the coffee pots out in the hallway for room service and took the elevator down to the lobby. The casino pulsated with the frenetic energy of tourists and locals intermingling one with another. Candy and I made our way past them and cocktail waitresses, who hurried about, serving slot machine players. The cacophony of the slot machines annoyed me, and the din didn't cease until Candy and I entered the parking garage, which felt like an oven turned on full blast.

I drove to Waxwell's building and parked trunk-end first in one of the visitor slots near an underground garage. I removed Eliot Waxwell's business card from my wallet and keyed in the number into my Samsung. I told Candy what to say. And, after Candy said it, she was to hang up, I said.

I pushed the dial button and handed the cell phone to Candy, who cupped it to her ear. I heard a phone ringing and then heard the secretary answer.

"This is Wang Min's office," Candy said. "You and your sister are in deep trouble. You'd better be at the gallery in the next twenty minutes, or else. And whatever you do, don't call."

Before the secretary could answer Candy, Candy hung up and handed the cell phone back to me.

"What's this about?" she said.

"I'm not sure yet. But if this new path is the correct one, we're on to something."

We waited in the Jetta, whose air conditioning I kept running. I watched the entrance-exit of the parking garage. Ten minutes passed, and Candy asked what I was waiting for. I told her that we needed to be a little more patient, and sure enough, after another two minutes or so, a car shot up the exit ramp and turned a corner, tires screeching. I saw that the driver was the vulpine secretary. She was wearing sunglasses, and her lips were pressed firmly together, making her look determined in a steely way. Her black Mini Cooper sped out of the parking lot, and I put the Jetta into drive and followed her, speeding to catch up with her.

"Who is that?" Candy said.

"An identical twin, the other part of a central piece in a puzzle missing several pieces."

"She killed Arthur?"

"I doubt it," I said. "But I believe that she's going to lead us to the person who did."

The secretary drove up a street, heading toward the Strip. I drove into an alley, turned onto another street, and drove as quickly as I could, without breaking the speed limit. Now was not the time to get pulled over by the cops.

"Where are we going?" Candy said.

"To the Miracle Mile Shops. She's going there to meet her twin sister, who manages the Jacobs Gallery. And from there, we'll play it by ear."

"I didn't think that you liked to play things by ear."

"I don't, but in this case, we don't have any other choice but to improvise."

I took side streets until I reached the Strip. On the Strip, I drove to the Planet Hollywood Casino, where I had valet park the Jetta. Taking Candy by the hand, I led her into the labyrinthine passageway of the shops. I hadn't walked that quickly in quite some time and was huffing and sweating. Candy strove to keep up with me. We passed tourists, and a security guard asked why we were in a hurry. I ignored him and kept moving.

Candy and I reached the end of the Miracle Mile Shops. The Jacobs Gallery had its doors open, welcoming us to enter.

"What now?" Candy said.

"We wait," I said and motioned for Candy to follow me.

We went into another shop—a high-end souvenir shop that sold overly priced trinkets and candies and shirts, all Las Vegas-themed—and I hung around the front, pretending that I was interested in stuffed animals wearing hats and T-shirts. A saleswoman attempted to engage me in a conversation, but Candy intervened and said that she was interested in purchasing a set of cutlery on the other side of the story. The chirpy saleswoman went to help Candy, and when I put a stuffed bear down, I saw that the secretary was entering the Jacobs Gallery, looking about frantically. She called out for Marie, and one of the viewing room doors opened, and out stepped Marie LeBeau, who closed the door behind her and who looked very puzzled as her twin sister gesticulated and spoke loudly. Marie LeBeau put a finger vertically to her lips, indicating that her sister should keep it down, but the secretary kept talking loudly and then grabbed Marie LeBeau by the lapels of Marie LeBeau's jacket and shook Marie LeBeau violently.

I stepped out of the high-end souvenir shop and headed into the Jacobs Gallery. The secretary was cussing, and an elderly couple emerged from the viewing room, looking bewildered. The couple quickly walked around the arguing sisters and exited the gallery, the woman saying that she would never, ever go to that gallery never, ever again. A salesman followed the elderly couple, imploring them to come back into the gallery.

"I wish that I could say that it was nice to see you again," I said to Marie LeBeau and her identical twin. "Unfortunately, it's not."

The two turned to me, and both glowered. The secretary raised her index finger.

Before she could say anything, I continued: "I know that you two are involved in something that's way above your heads, the necks of which, by the way, are on chopping blocks. Now, I suggest that we go to the back of the gallery, out of view of the security camera, and have a calm, rational talk about what you've been doing for Eliot Waxwell and Wang Min. After this talk, I'll decide if I should call the feds and keep you here until they arrive."

The secretary looked at Marie, and Marie looked at the secretary. Then they looked at me, nodded, and turned, leading the way to the back of the gallery. Marie told the salesman that she would be back in a few moments, and that we—she, her sister, and I—were not to be disturbed.

There, in a work area in the back of the gallery, Marie LeBeau and her identical twin crossed their arms in perfect sync. I leaned back against a large, empty frame and studied the secretary, then Marie LeBeau.

"How long have you been playing Waxwell and Wang?" I said. "And what are you hoping to get out of it?"

Marie looked at her sister and then looked at me.

"How did you know?" Marie said.

"It wasn't that difficult," I said. "For starters, Zsa Zsa Cortez doesn't know anything at all about mathematics. You made it sound as if he was a mathematical genius like Arthur Vogel. If Zsa Zsa could do basic algebra, that would be saying a lot. The point is, only someone who knew about mathematics would speak the way that you spoke." I looked at the secretary. "As for you, well, you made the mistake of doing your work at your workstation. I could tell that the formulas that you were entering into that spreadsheet were far beyond the average secretary's grasp. I know enough about mathematics to know that you were working at a very advanced level, say, postdoctoral. What's more, the speed at which you were doing your work showed that you'd done this type of work for quite some time."

Marie LeBeau stepped back, and I raised my hands, just in case she attempted to reach for a utility knife that was lying on a table littered with catalogs and mailers. Seeing my reaction, she lowered her hand. Her twin sister removed her sunglasses.

"So," I said, "what angles are you playing against Waxwell and Wang?"

"That's none of your business," Marie LeBeau's identical twin said, and she said a few other things before Marie told her to calm down.

"Is your real name Marie?" I said to Marie LeBeau.

"It is," Marie said, staring at me, and I wasn't sure if she felt anger or hatred at that moment. "And my sister is Calais."

"You have a choice, Marie and Calais, and this is my final offer. You tell me what's going on, or I'm going to call the feds and hold you both here until they arrive."

Marie LeBeau sighed and removed her spinster's reading glasses from her face, allowing her glasses to dangle from their chain on her narrow chest.

"It's like this," she said, after a few moments had passed. "We're getting revenge."

"What did Waxwell and Wang do to you?"

"Our parents," Calais said. "They killed our parents."

"What?" I said. "Why would they do that?"

"You'd have to know our story to understand," Marie said. "We were born in Romania, to a father of French descent and to a mother of Romanian descent. Our parents were engineering professors in Bucharest and took us out of Romania after Ceausescu's execution, when we were finally able to escape. We moved to Paris, where we lived for quite some time and where Calais and I received most of our formal schooling. It was there, in Paris, where our parents discovered that my sister and I were mathematical geniuses."

"What was your area of expertise?" I said. "Computer algorithms? Security? Networking?"

"No," Calais said, looking perplexed. "We absolutely had no interest in those things."

"Absolutely not," Marie said, and she had a strange smile on her face, as if she were reminiscing about a very pleasant past. "No, both of us had—have—a passion for randomness."

"I've never heard of you. Why wouldn't the media cover such two mathematical prodigies?"

"Our parents protected us as best they could," Calais said. "Part of that protection was keeping us shielded from all media, which, for the most part, they detested. They refused to read newspapers or to watch television. They definitely hated

Hollywood films and what they considered the decadence of Hollywood. As you can imagine, when my sister and I weren't studying mathematics, we were being schooled in the classics or taking ballet classes. Our parents loved ballet, and they had a passion for symphonies, especially the Russian ones and any work by Orff or Puccini. As you can see, we led a very cloistered life."

"I understand what a cloistered life is like," I said. "I was a Benedictine monk several years ago."

"Oh?" Calais raised an eyebrow. "Where?"

"Fontgombault Abbey, in France."

"Interesting," Marie said. "You do seem to have a clerical property about you."

I looked over Marie LeBeau's shoulder at one of Zsa Zsa's paintings, which was being readied for a frame. The painting seemed to suggest that it was a study about confusion, but, if anything, this artwork, if it could be called that, was about the so-called artist's own confusion.

Then I said, "Please, go on with your story. I'd like to hear why Waxwell and Wang murdered your parents."

"We excel at anything having to do with randomness," Calais said. "We even wrote papers on it, and the NSA and other US governmental agencies contacted our parents, asking if they would be willing to come to this country. Our parents, who were having financial hardship in Paris, decided to come to the United States, and so we moved to Baltimore, where Marie and I finished our formal education at Johns Hopkins."

I looked into the gallery, which was vacant, and then returned my attention to the identical twins. "So, how does Eliot Waxwell play into this?"

"One of Eliot Waxwell's companies was doing business with the NSA," Marie said. "He heard of our talent and approached our parents, asking them if they would allow us to work for his company. My parents refused because they didn't trust him. Two weeks later, our parents were coming home to Baltimore from Washington DC, after attending a concert at the French embassy. Their car ran off the highway and struck a tree and exploded."

"And you're sure that Waxwell was responsible for his?" I said. "If so, how?"

"They died just like that journalist in Los Angeles, the one who worked for *Rolling Stone* magazine," Calais said, and she stared at a far wall. I wondered what she saw there. "We know that they were murdered by Waxwell because two weeks later, we were living at his home in Atlanta, Georgia, and working for his company. We were fourteen at the time, and he had full, legal guardianship over us."

"I find that hard to believe," I said. "For one thing, adoption through the courts can take a year or more. Didn't you have relatives with whom you could stay? And didn't anybody see through his ruse?"

Marie and Calais laughed. "You obviously don't understand the powers that the powers that be have," Marie said. "If one of the elite wants something, they get it. Eliot Waxwell has pull not only with the NSA, but with the CIA, the FBI, the DoD, and several other acronyms."

"Did he abuse you, other than having your parents murdered?"

"Never," Calais said. "He was rarely around. He was constantly traveling around the world, and when he wasn't doing that, he was in Las Vegas. Marie and I talked one night about committing suicide, because our situation seemed so hopeless. But we decided that committing suicide would be admitting that Waxwell had won a moral victory. So, we chose to live. We finished our post-doctoral work in Atlanta, while working for his company, which, when it all comes down to it, was the NSA."

"And what, exactly, were you doing?"

Marie and Calais looked at each other, silently communicating in the way in which only identical twins can communicate. Then they both turned slowly to me. Calais motioned for Marie to speak.

"We were narrowing down randomness," Marie said. "Or, in other words, learning how to corral randomness by narrowing its influences further and further. Using several thousand databases and servers, we were able to determine what occurred in a country because of a given political situation or what have you. Many people, of course, make predictions about what's going to happen. But these are predictions. They might or might not come true, and, if they do, well, more often than not, the predictions aren't accurate.

"But because my sister and I can analyze billions of bits of data and come up with flow patterns and stochastic determinations, as we call them, we can show what will occur in Brazil on Friday with the sugar futures, or what the exact price Microsoft's stock will be on a Monday morning after the CEO announces the layoff of two thousand employees, or what the price of gasoline will be in Platina, California, if two drone strikes occur in Yemen." She paused. "My sister and I, as you can see, have made it possible for Eliot Waxwell to 'make' his billions, among other things."

"That's impossible," I said. "If it were true, why weren't you able to see my coming into the picture?"

"Because we didn't have any data pertaining to you," Calais said. "As my sister and I will tell you, we don't control randomness, we just do our best to corral it. My sister and I have perfected our mathematical skills to the point where we're only one ten-thousandth off." Calais paused, to create an effect. "That's not perfect, of course, but it's close enough, wouldn't you agree, Mr. Fitzpatrick?"

I scratched my shaved chin and shook my head. My head was swimming. It felt like being in a universe created by Philip K. Dick; you believed that you were living reality in a real world, but after the veil was pulled back, you saw that you had been living in an unreal universe, one run by a malevolent deity who had been doing nothing but playing games with you.

"Three questions come to mind," I said. "First, why haven't the agents of foreign governments absconded with you or had you killed? Second, why hasn't the US government done that?"

"Waxwell has agreements with politicians and representatives of the US government," Calais said. "Waxwell has, let us say, information that could destroy quite a few political lives, including that of the president. In other words, they fear Waxwell, and they know that if they provoke him or do anything to him, they, too, are going to go down. He doesn't control all aspects of the government, of course, especially the rogues, whom he greatly fears. But so far, my sister and I have been able to keep him protected because of our own needs and purposes.

"As for your former question, well, we're an urban legend among foreign governments and spies. We're like the mermaids or the Sasquatches of cryptozoology. People want to believe in us, but they can't because once they see what we can do, their biases won't allow them to see the truth. Two Mossad agents, for instance, took an interest in my sister and me but went back to their country empty-handed, not believing what they had seen. Marie and I are certain that they told the Israeli government that we were nothing but the figment of some senile politician's imagination."

"You said that you had a third question," Marie said. "What is it?"

"Where does Wang come into all of this? You said that he and Waxwell were both responsible for the murder of your parents."

"Wang came to Waxwell with a business proposition, shortly before our parents were murdered," Marie said. "Wang, as you know, owns an international shipping company. But what you probably don't know is that it's not the shipments from this legitimate company that have made him a magnate, contrary to what *Forbes* and the *Wall Street Journal* and *USA Today* might have us to believe. It's his other shipping activities, which he's been doing for years, that have made him his billions."

I looked at Marie, then at Calais, and then back at Marie. They had very truthful faces. They would have made bad championship-level poker players.

"Wang needed a way to ensure that his shipments wouldn't be intercepted by customs or the border patrol," Calais said. "There is, of course, a lot of money at stake in this one particular market. I don't think that either my sister or I need to tell you what this market is."

No, they didn't need to tell me. I knew what it was, and I knew that Marie and Calais had been plotting routes for traffickers and computing when it was the best time for shipments to be brought in from Mexico, Canada, or on the coasts. Waxwell had been using Zsa Zsa Cortez's so-called art, among other things, to launder drug money.

"So, how are you going to get your revenge?" I said.

"We won't tell you," Marie said.

"That's for us to know and only us," Calais said.

"You two could be in very serious trouble," I said, "and not because of me or because of the feds. You do know that you two are a liability to Waxwell and Wang, don't you? I met with Waxwell this morning, and believe me, he's not the type of man who will go to prison without taking several people with him. You two are the ones who could easily have him and Wang sent away. What makes you think Waxwell will let you live? After all, I was closing in on him, and he was about to come undone. He's suspicious and very fearful. What if he snaps?"

"He won't kill us because Wang needs us," Calais said. "Wang's a very egotistical man, as you probably know. He believes that he's invincible. He wants us to continue plotting the pathways and goings-on of the border patrol and coast guard, until the situation becomes so tenuous that he has to pull out, like a fighter pilot heading straight toward a mountain and then veering off at the last microsecond."

"If you're thinking about murdering them, I wouldn't do it," I said. "It won't bring you satisfaction, at least not ultimately."

"We're not murderers like Waxwell and Wang, Mr. Fitzpatrick," Marie said. "You don't need to bring that up any further."

The salesman appeared, asking if we were done because Mr. Jacobs had just called and was coming into the gallery, and Marie knew, of course, that Mr. Jacobs didn't like it when his employees had friends or visitors in the gallery, didn't she?

Marie replied that we were done, and then she and her sister spoke in French, and, seeing that I understood them, switched to what sounded like Romanian. I thought about asking them more questions but decided that it was pointless.

I left the back area and walked through the gallery. Zsa Zsa's red, black, and white paintings assaulted my eyes. I wanted to get out of the gallery and out to a quiet place, preferably a cool, dimly lit room, where I could rest my senses.

Candy was sitting on a wooden bench across from the Jacobs Gallery, into which a wizened, little, spavined man hurried. He called out to Marie in a screechy voice, and I didn't have to be told that this was Mr. Jacobs.

I sat down next to Candy.

"Was the lead correct?" she said.

I nodded. "It is, but there's more to the story."

"Like what?"

"I'm not sure yet, Candy. The important thing is that we now have the base of the puzzle. Now we just need to find the smaller, missing parts and get them connected."

Then Candy and I exited the labyrinthine Miracle Mile Shops. Candy said that she wanted to have lunch and said that she knew of a good place at the Paris. I said that I didn't want to hear about Paris, and when Candy replied with a puzzled look, I took her by the hand and said that we would have lunch at the Bellagio.

Sixteen

I took Candy back to the Orleans Casino. I put the battery into my Samsung and checked my messages. I had one, and it was from Maxine, who asked me to call her as soon as I got her message.

"What's going on, Max?" I said.

"Where are you, Fitz?"

"What does it matter?"

"Have you seen the news?"

"No, I haven't, and I haven't listened to the radio or gone on the Internet," I said. "What is it?"

Candy had gone up to the room, and I was standing in an alcove near a new food court, where I purchasing a Starbucks decaf Americano.

She sighed. "You're not going to believe this."

"I'll believe about anything at this time," I said, and I took my change and receipt from the barista, thanked her, and then dropped coins into a small, Plexiglas tip jar. I walked away from the counter and out a side door because the casino's din was too loud. A squawk of static came over the line, sounding as if Maxine and I were cut off. "You there, Max?"

"Yes, I'm here." She paused. "Eliot Waxwell is dead."

Out in the parking lot, a wiry man, sporting a blond-going-to-gray mustache and wearing a black, ten-gallon hat, carried two overly stuffed suitcases while a morbidly obese woman followed, huffing and puffing like a struggling engine.

"Fitz?"

"Why are you telling me this, Max?"

"Because of what you're doing here in Las Vegas." There was a long, uneasy pause. "We can't prove it, but we think that you were at the warehouse last night, right before it burned down. But we do know that his morning, you went to Eliot Waxwell's offices on Howard Hughes Parkway."

I didn't answer.

"Fitz?"

"How was he killed, Max?"

"Gunned down," she said. "Him and his two bodyguards, right there in his suite. Why did you visit Eliot Waxwell this morning, Fitz?"

"You're trying to bait me, Max. Please don't do it, unless you want to end what little of our friendship remains."

She sighed. "I need to speak to you right now."

"Why?"

"Why do you think, Fitz?" She sounded very irritated, and I felt very irritated. "You either speak to me, or Larsen and his people are coming for you. And, if you want me to make it worse, I'll sic Mankowski on you."

"You've got me there," I said. "Larsen I can barely stomach, Mankowski, not. But I have to say, if we keep meeting like this, people are going to talk."

She said that she was in town and could meet me anywhere that I liked. I suggested the Sunset Station Casino, down in Henderson, and said that I would meet her there in forty-five minutes at the sports book.

After I finished speaking with Maxine, I gave Lenny a call and asked him to send someone down to the Orleans to wait for me at the valet station.

Candy was lying on the bed, sleeping peacefully, when I entered the room. I closed the door gently behind me and sat down on the bed next to her. Spots on her pillow showed that she had been crying before she fell asleep. She startled awake, and I told her that it was okay, and she smiled and looked up at me, her platinum-colored hair tumbling into her eyes and their beautiful, ice blue irides. She looked so innocent, the way Marilyn Monroe had. I could see why Arthur had fallen in love with her.

"I was having a pleasant dream," she said. "Arthur was alive and happy, and we were driving on a highway in California, a highway that was like a rollercoaster, and we were both laughing and enjoying the ride." She blinked. "I think we were going to Yosemite."

"I'm going to Henderson," I said. "Maxine wants to meet with me."

"Oh, to hell with Maxine." Candy stretched and yawned and then curled up on the bed like a content cat. She closed her eyes. "All she does is call you."

"Candy—"

"Let me stay here, Frank," she said, yawning. "I'm so tired. And I'll be all right, I promise."

"There's too much bad stuff going on. A friend of a friend is coming over to pick you up and take you away."

"Where?" she said, yawning.

"I don't know," I said, "and I don't want to know. If someone captures me and they torture me, I won't be able to tell them."

"Quit joking, Frank."

"I'm not joking, Candy," I said, and I forced her sit up. "I just spoke with Maxine a few minutes ago. Eliot Waxwell is dead, and she—"

"Eliot Waxwell is dead?"

"That's what Maxine said," and I helped Candy stand. "The friend should be here now. Get your things. You're going on a road trip."

In the reception area, I gave Candy the money that Zsa Zsa had given to me and the cell phone that I had used to take photos of the slain ephebes and of the two men whom I had knocked out and bound. Outside, I saw Candy off at the valet station, and the souped-up Mustang in which she was riding shot westward on Tropicana Avenue, heading toward the sun. And then I retrieved the Jetta and drove south on the 95 to Henderson.

At the Sunset Station Casino, I dropped off my car with a valet and entered the casino and walked to the sports book. A skinny-legged waitress walked quickly around me, and an old man sitting at a slot machine coughed, as if he were hacking up his lungs, and then took another drag off a cheap stogie dripping from his fingers.

Maxine was sitting in front of a monitor in the sports book. She was wearing a beige shirt and beige pants and black pumps, looking very serious and businesslike. She was studying screens on the wall across from the station where she was sitting. Several of the screens showed horse races and dog races already in progress. Stats appeared on a neon board, showing the results of recent baseball games and other sporting events. The air smelled like steamed hot dogs, which a vendor standing behind a cart was hawking to hungry-looking people.

I looked at her and then at the bettors, most of whom were men in their sixties and beyond, studying racing forms or studying monitors. One man threw up his racing form in obvious disgust and stormed out of the sports book, heading my direction and cussing under his breath. I maneuvered around him.

I sat down in a chair next to Maxine's. She swiveled in her chair to face me, her arms crossed, the expression on her face Grim Reaper serious.

"It's always good to see you when you're so happy," I said. I feigned a smile. "So, here I am, Max. What shall we talk about today?"

"Why did you go see Eliot Waxwell?" Her jaw muscles tensed.

"You first, Max. What's the story behind Waxwell's murder?"

"A janitor found Waxwell and his two bodyguards in Waxwell's suite. All of them had been shot point-blank from behind, indicating that they were execution-style murders. Now, why did you go see Eliot Waxwell, Fitz?"

"That's my business, not yours."

"Didn't I tell you that we were doing an operation?" she said. "Didn't I tell you to leave him alone? What don't you understand?"

"The overall picture is still recondite, but I'm beginning to understand more and more," I said. "And, actually, Eliot Waxwell wanted to see me. He wanted to see what I knew about him. And what I knew about him was way off."

"What did he want to know, Fitz?"

"Why should I tell you?" I said.

A buxom cocktail waitress, whose tanned cleavage threatened to spill out of her uniform, asked if we wanted something to drink, and I ordered a bottle of chilled water, which I asked the waitress to serve to me capped. Maxine ordered a gin and tonic. The waitress moved on.

Then I continued: "If your position on the chessboard is the way mine was, you're way, way off. There's more to this than meets the eye."

"That's why I asked to meet with you," she said. "You know what we need to know. So, tell me what it is you know."

"Perhaps you should be speaking with Wang Min. After all, isn't he the logical suspect in all of this?"

"Wang Min's in Macao."

"Investigate his friends, then," I said. "I'm sure that they might have a few interesting things to say about their whereabouts and goings-on."

"We might investigate you, Fitz. As I said, we suspect that you were at that warehouse last night. Did you know the victims?"

I studied her a moment, trying to determine if she was being level or playing a game with me. I surmised that it might be both, so I decided to play it safe. "I might be acquainted with them, whoever they were." I blinked. "Do you know who they were, Max?"

"Three of what appear to be Zsa Zsa's boys," Maxine said. "The bodies were burned beyond recognition, so we're relying on dental records. From the looks of things, they were dead before the fire began. Do you know who might have done that, Fitz?"

The buxom cocktail waitress placed a straw and a paper coaster in front of me. Then she placed a bottle of water onto the coaster; the bottle had been cracked open. Then the cocktail waitress placed a gin and tonic, along with a coaster, in front of Maxine. I handed the cocktail waitress two crisp bills, for which she thanked me. She then hurried off to serve bettors.

"I plead the Fifth," I said.

Maxine leaned in close. "You listen to me, and you listen good, Fitz," she said. "I'm tired of your games. We know that you were there, and we know that two Asian men were there. We can't find them, though we suspect that they were working for Wang Min. Obviously, they wanted to destroy something in that ware-house, and it wasn't those stupid, overpriced paintings."

"Perhaps," I said, wanting to see how much further I could bait her without her exploding.

"Take a look around, Fitz."

I did. None of the people in the sports books noticed them, but men in dark suits were standing near cocktail stations and slot machines, looking at Maxine and me. She didn't have to tell me who they were. I thought I saw Larsen among the slot machines, but it turned out to be a tall, gaunt man who looked dejected.

"So?"

"If I don't get the information that I need, they're going to get it for me."

"You know that I don't like threats, Max."

"I don't care, Fitz," and she said a string of words that were printable in our age but unprintable in more civilized ones. "Believe me, it won't be pretty."

And I knew that it wouldn't be. I had played it straight with Eliot Waxwell; I decided to take my chances and play it straight with Maxine and see where it went.

"All right," I said, "I went to speak to Eliot Waxwell about the fire at the warehouse."

"Why?"

"Because I thought that he and Wang Min were responsible. I wanted to find out if Waxwell knew anything or might even confess to anything."

"Not likely, Fitz, but I'm sure you did your best to get an answer from him. Why was that fire of interest to you?"

"Because I was there, before it started," I said. "In fact, I made the call to 911, not about the fire but about the three slain ephebes. They had been murdered, and two men, two Chinese, were going to torch down the warehouse studio before I knocked them out and tied them up. Someone obviously let them go or helped them to escape. Given that the cops and the fire department were on their way, I'd suspect one of those two. But if I was to wager," I said, continuing, "I would put my money down on the cops."

She nodded at the bottle of water. "Aren't you going to drink?"

"I don't think so."

"Afraid that we're going to poison you, Fitz?"

"Or worse. You've already threatened me. And I know what your people are capable of, so why shouldn't I be extra cautious?"

She smirked. "Speaking of being extra cautious, did you get any evidence from the warehouse?"

"I took photos."

"Are they on your cell phone?"

"No, they're not," I said. "And even if they were, do you think I'd have them there without making copies? Rest assured, I have evidence, and I have it hidden in several geographic locations."

"You were always one for being prepared, weren't you, Fitz?"

"Of course, Max. Unprepared people often meet untimely deaths."

"Good point." She sipped her gin and tonic. "Now that you told me about the warehouse, I'm willing to open up to you. Do you have any questions?"

"Several, but I'll ask the relevant few. For starters, who else besides Waxwell and his two bodyguards were gunned down?"

"Nobody."

"What about the security guards up front? Or Waxwell's secretary?"

"The guards are fine. Everyone else in that building is fine. As for the admin, we can't find her. She is, of course, a person of interest."

"You won't find her."

"Why not?"

"You wouldn't believe it if I told you," I said. "Anything caught on the security cameras?"

"Waxwell wouldn't allow them on his floor," she said. "More than likely, he didn't want anything recorded that could be used against him."

"What about the entry logs at the front desk?"

"You were his last visitor," she said. "At least officially, that is."

"Which makes me a suspect, at least in the eyes of the Las Vegas PD, among others."

"Of course." She finished her drink; ice cubes clacked against her teeth, and she set the glass down on top of the coaster the cocktail waitress had placed near the base of the monitor. Maxine chewed one of the ice cubes. "One question about slipped my mind."

"That's all right," I said. "I'm tired of answering questions."

"What happened to Zsa Zsa? You must know where he is, Fitz."

"No, I don't know where he is," I said, standing. "I'm going to leave now. Your friends might decide to follow me, and, if they do, that's their business. But, if they attempt to overtake me, I'm going to fight. You might want to tell them that."

Maxine frowned and shook her head. "Why can't you ever be reasonable, Fitz?"

"I'm very reasonable," I said, turning. "Unfortunately, it's the rest of the world that fails to be."

Seventeen

I tipped the valet two dollars for bringing me the Jetta, and he thanked me and bade me a good day. I headed south on the 95, wanting to see if I was being tailed. It looked as if a black Lincoln Town Car with tinted windows might be following me, but when I slowed down, the vehicle went into the left lane, speeding past me and ripping toward the southern outskirts of Henderson. I took an exit, at which billboards advertised the services of DUI lawyers. In the parking lot of a megachurch that looked like a smaller version of Eliot Waxwell's office building, I waited to see if anyone would show up. No one did. Then I turned around, got onto an entry ramp, and headed north on the 95, speeding past the Valley Auto Mall and other businesses along the way.

At the 95 and 15 interchange, I took the 15, heading north, until I reached Craig Road, whose exit I took. I drove past the Cannery Casino, and a few minutes later, I parked the Jetta in front of the North Las Vegas house that Jonathan Beard had shared with Kack.

The house looked as it did during my previous visit, except that the garage door was up. Kack's corroded teal Corolla was parked in the garage. Next to the Corolla sat the dusty, Arctic blue dune buggy that I had seen during my previous visit. I walked up the flagstone steps to the front door and knocked and then stepped back, not wanting to crowd the stucco doorframe.

I heard someone at the front door, sensed their looking at me through the spy glass, and then the front door opened. Kack was standing there, a Nordstrom shopping bag full of stuffed animals in hand. She was wearing yellow-framed sunglasses and red, baggy shorts and a pink T-shirt decaled with a smiling baby elephant holding an umbrella.

"Jonathan's not here," she said. "And I can't tell you where he is. I just got here an hour ago. I'm packing and moving back to LA."

"He told me that you were," I said. "Mind if I come in?"

"I don't think I'd wait around for him, mister. Sometimes he goes away for days at a time."

"I need to tell you something about Jonathan, Kack."

"Oh?"

I nodded. She invited me inside. I stepped inside, and she closed the door behind us, locking the door. I walked into the living room, where Jonathan and I had spoken, and sat down on the lacerated, leather sofa. I glanced over my shoulder at the blood-smeared wall into which I had rammed Jonathan's face three times. The room was redolent of vanilla incense.

Kack placed the shopping bag full of stuffed animals down beside the La-Z-Boy but sat on the edge of the sofa. The soles of her bare feet were besooted from, I assumed, walking on the unwashed, tessellated floors.

"So, what did you want to tell me, mister?"

"It's Frank, Frank Fitzpatrick," I said. "And I might as well cut to the chase, Kack." I cleared my throat, which was irritated after having been exposed to cigarette smoke at the Sunset Station Casino. "Jonathan is dead."

She blinked. Then sighed. Those were her only outward responses. I couldn't know, of course, what she was thinking or feeling.

"How did it happen?"

"Before I can answer that question, you need to know what Jonathan was doing." I paused to let her know that I was being deadly serious. "Can you handle the truth, Kack?"

She nodded.

And for the next few minutes, I told her about Arthur and Candy and about why I had come to Las Vegas and about what I knew about Jonathan and his relationship with the two other ephebes and with Zsa Zsa Cortez. And then I told her about how I had found Jonathan and the other ephebes at the warehouse studio and how I had startled the two men who had seemingly murdered the ephebes and who were obviously going to burn the place to the ground.

"At first, I thought that they were going to burn down the warehouse studio to hide something," I said. "Now I believe it might be otherwise."

"Like what?"

"That, perhaps, the two men weren't after something but after someone and not necessarily Zsa Zsa Cortez," I said. "I think that Jonathan knew more than he was letting on and he attacked me, not only because he thought that I doubted his heterosexuality but because he thought I might come on to something that implicated him in Arthur Vogel's murder."

Kack rubbed a besooted foot. "Where did this friend of yours die?"

"No one knows. They found his body at an abandoned motel on Harmon, down the street from the Hard Rock. But a morgue attendant at the coroner's said that Arthur had been dead a few days when they found the body. And, what's more, someone in the coroner's office discovered that Arthur's corpse had radioactive particles on it."

"Why would it have those?"

"That's what I'm attempting to discover," I said. "Arthur worked at the Nevada Test Site, where there's a lot of radioactive material. The thing is, there are detectors at the front gates, which are the only authorized way into and out of the Test Site. And those detectors can detect the minutest hints of radioactive material. One time, for example, a man who'd had heart trouble and who'd gone to a doctor was pulled aside after he attempted to enter the Test Site. It seemed that he'd undergone nuclear testing of some sort. That's how sensitive those detectors are. So, if Arthur Vogel had had traces of radioactive materials on him, why didn't the detectors at the front gates go off?"

Kack shrugged and then crossed one leg over the other. She was now sitting in a full lotus position.

"When was the last time that Jonathan or you used that dune buggy in the garage?"

"I think Jonathan took it out last week," she said, "but I'm not sure. Why?"

"Do you have a clean pillow case or a clean bath towel that I could use?"

"Yeah, I do." She seemed puzzled. "What are you doing to do?"

"Get me one of those items, Kack, and I'll show you."

She went into one of the back rooms and came out with a purple terrycloth towel, which she handed to me and for which I thanked her. I then told her that I was going into the garage to do a test. She followed. In the sweltering garage, I inspected the dune buggy for signs of blood or tissue, but I didn't find anything. I ran the purple terrycloth towel around the dune buggy, ensuring that I covered every square inch. And then I opened the freezer, which was empty and pleasantly cold, and ran the towel around its cold interior.

Then I went back inside, and Kack followed, closing the garage door and locking it behind us. I picked up a Smith's plastic bag, into which I placed the towel.

"What were you doing in there?" she said.

"Seeing if there's any radioactive residue. As I said, I've a reasonable suspicion that Jonathan was involved in Arthur Vogel's murder. If so, Jonathan could have used the dune buggy to transport the body to town."

"Care for a beer?"

"No, thank you, Kack."

"You a reformed alcoholic or something?"

"Not at all. I just never liked the taste of alcohol."

"Suit yourself."

She opened a refrigerator door and removed a bottle of Corona, which she uncapped. She closed the refrigerator door.

"I have one question," I said.

"What?"

"Are you going to live the rest of your life this way, Kack, moving from one loser to another?"

She smirked. "I don't think that's any of your business."

"You're right, Kack, it's not. But you're smart, street-wise, at least. You could lead a better life, if you chose to do so."

She laughed. Her laughter was loud and arrogant and joyful and full of life and larger than life, the complete opposite of the elfin mystique that she projected.

"Well, for your information, I'm going back to LA to live with my parents. I'm going to attend a community college and study computers." She drained the beer and then dropped the bottle into a trash receptacle full of empty beer bottles and cigarette butts and ash and debris. "I'm going to make big money and give up the party lifestyle. Satisfied with that answer, Frank?"

"I believe you," I said. "I really do. And, for what it's worth, I'm satisfied."

"I need to finish packing," she said. "I don't want to be in this house any longer, especially now."

She walked me to the front door, where I thanked her and went to my Jetta, plastic bag in hand. The sun had reddened on the horizon, and if I had been a sailor, I would have taken that as a good omen.

But I wasn't a sailor. So, I drove off without a good omen, knowing that I had much, much more work to do.

Eighteen

I called Al the morgue attendant on his cell phone and asked him how things were going. He said that he'd won a cool grand the other day at Caesar's Palace and said that I needed to get back into handicapping.

"You gotta move out here to Las Vegas," he said. "You and me, we could make a killing. I could leave this godforsaken job and live the life of Raleigh or whatever the hell they call it, and you, you could be there right along beside me."

"You working?"

"Unfortunately, yeah, I am."

"I'd like to swing by. I have a favor to ask of you. Actually, two."

"What are they?"

"We'll discuss them when I get there."

"Yeah, right, right."

I parked on the street and met him at the smoking area. I told him that I wanted him to test the purple blanket for radioactive particles and then to come back and give me his findings. Al the morgue attendant agreed, took the towel from me, and then went back into the building. While he was gone, I checked my cell phone messages, deleting one from an insurance agent who wouldn't take the hint that my not returning his calls meant that I didn't want to do business with him.

Al the morgue attendant returned about ten minutes later with the purple terrycloth blanket, which he handed to me.

"What did you discover?" I said.

"Same readings." He lit a cigarette, and he seemed greasier than he did before. "Minute traces, all right. Probably from the same source, you ask me."

"That's what I'm thinking."

"Was that Arthur Vogel's blanket?"

"No," I said, and I stepped back, away from the cigarette smoke that was twirling around Al the morgue attendant's head and threatening to snake its way toward me. "It belongs to a friend of mine. What's important is not to whom it belonged but what's on it."

"Where did it end up getting those radioactive particles?"

"On a vehicle that appears as if it was used to transport Arthur Vogel's body," I said, placing the purple terrycloth towel into the Smith's plastic bag. "I have one other thing to ask you."

"Oh, yeah, right, right, the other favor."

"When are they going to do the autopsies on Eliot Waxwell and his two bodyguards?"

"First thing tomorrow morning." He blinked and then took a short drag off his cigarette. "Why?"

"I was wondering what caliber the bullets were." I turned and headed back to the Jetta. "Talk with you later."

"Hey," he said, calling out to me.

I stopped and turned. "What?"

"What about some more handicapping?" He held out a racing form. "You going to pick some more winners for me?"

"Let me know the caliber of the bullets used to kill Eliot Waxwell and his bodyguards, and we'll talk," I said. "Until then, goodbye."

He waved his hand in disgust at me and threw his cigarette down onto the pavement and ground the life out of the cigarette with a heel of a black oxford. "Have a good night yourself."

He stormed away, and I turned around and headed back to the Jetta.

🍎

I drove to the Orleans Casino, where I had valet park the Jetta. I called room service and ordered a steak, cooked rare, and two helpings of steamed broccoli. Then I called Lenny to check on things. After I hung up, I made calls to friends in Florida to see how things were at my beachfront condo. A few minutes later, there was a knock on the door, and it was room service with my dinner. I tipped the server, only to discover, a couple of minutes later, that my steak had been cooked until it was well-done. I begrudgingly ate my dinner and then kicked off my Converses and lay back on the bed, staring up at the ceiling.

I felt enervated and wanted to sleep, but the sleep wouldn't come. So, I got up, turned down the lights, and watched the local evening news. The top story, of course, was the murder of Eliot Waxwell. The elderly, rheumy-eyed security guard appeared onscreen, and he spoke in a shaky voice, while a reporter grilled him about who the killer might be. Before turning off the television set, I postulated that the security guard would quit his job and go into a safer line of work, like dealing blackjack at one of the station casinos around town.

Then I showered and, still not able to sleep, dressed and decided that I would go down to the casino. In an elevator, I ran into the wiry man with the black, ten-gallon hat. His blond-going-to-gray mustache twitched, and the obese woman who had followed him into the casino was standing beside him, huffing and puffing, as if she'd finished sprinting thirty yards. The man nodded at me, and I nodded back, and then he took and held the hand of the obese woman as the elevator continued its smooth descent to the casino floor.

I went to a bar and sat down at a video poker game. The bartender asked me what I'd have, and I told him a soda water and lime. He told me soda water and lime it was and prepared my drink, while I fed a ten dollar bill into a slot next to the screen of the video poker game. Nearby, a hooting woman who looked like a six-foot-tall version of Tammy Faye Bakker jumped up and down, obviously happy with her roll at a craps table. Slot machines whirred and chirped. On balustrades overlooking the casino floor, motley attired mannequins, illuminated by colored footlights, peered down, as if the mannequins were enjoying a Bourbon Street Mardi Gras scene.

The bartender gave me my drink, I paid and tipped him, and then I played a couple of hands of video poker. When I looked up for a split second, something at the corner of my eye caught my attention. I turned quickly to see the back of Junior as he hurried past a slot machine. I frowned. Junior's being there meant that Mankowski was about. Which, obviously, meant that they knew that I was there.

I turned to play another hand of poker and sensed someone's standing behind me. I reached down and tapped my Samsung.

"Have a seat, Mankowski," I said, continuing to play my game. "Ask me a few questions, if you want, and, depending upon my mood, I'll decide if I'm going to answer them or not."

Mankowski sat down in a chair to my left; Junior slipped into the chair to my right.

"I'll buy you a Shirley Temple if you just keep your mouth shut," I said, turning to Junior and then turning to Mankowski, who was lighting one of his godawful Merits. "You can either put out that cigarette now, or I'm leaving."

Mankowski made a face and snubbed out the noxious cigarette.

"What are you doing here?" I said, starting another hand of video poker. I was up a little over two dollars and intended to keep it that way. "And how did you find me?"

"Just hanging out, looking for old friends," Mankowski said. "And look what we found here in this dinner of inequality, our old friend, Frank Fitzpatrick."

"That's den of iniquity." I turned to Junior, whose mouth was slightly open, looking as if he'd been stumped by the $64,000 question. "Can you believe the insipid malapropisms that your senior partner comes up with, Junior?"

"It's not Junior, it's Detective Farrell to you. I'm tired of this Junior crap." He looked like a sour kid whose team had just lost a T-ball championship.

"That's nice to know," I said. "Nice, shiny suit, by the way. Perhaps you can graduate to a belt from suspenders after you finish the third grade—"

"Hey, buddy—"

"What we want to know," Mankowski said, "is when you're going to solve the Arthur Vogel case, maybe even the Eliot Waxwell case."

"I bet you do. Now, tell me how you found me."

"That lady friend of yours told us, who else?"

"Petty revenge," I said. I lost the hand and pushed a graphical button to be dealt new cards.

"We're serious here, Fitzpatrick. We want to know when you're going to solve these cases."

I turned to Mankowski but didn't say anything.

"I know what you're thinking," Mankowski said. "You're wondering why we, of all people, would come to someone like you. Well, I hate to admit it, pal, but you're the only thing we got going for us. You help us, we'll help you."

"How?" I said. "By not arresting me again? Or by not beating the living tar out of me?"

Mankowski smirked in his babyish way and chewed the end of his mustache. His burnsides twitched. I could tell that what few gears he had in his head were turning, and he was doing his best to come up with an answer or with a question that would get him what he wanted.

"And why do you need my help?" I said, returning my attention back to the video poker game. I pushed a button, and the game dealt me my cards. "And what's in it for you?" I smiled; perhaps I was going to have a full house. "And, more important, what's in it for me?"

The bartender asked if I wanted a refill, to which I said yes. He poured it for me, I paid and tipped him, and then the bartender asked Mankowski and Junior what they were going to have. Mankowski ordered Cokes for him and Junior.

"Police work is a business," Junior said, after the bartender left. "We don't make a quota, they bring the heat down on us." He took a sip of his Coke. "It's been a bad year for my partner and me."

"Sounds as if you're working in sales," I said, "on a commission-only basis. That being the case, why don't you do what cops do and frame someone?"

"We tried—"

"Shut up," Mankowski said a little bit too loudly, trembling, thrusting his index finger at his partner. "I do the talking, understand?"

A henna-haired woman across the bar stared at us, afraid, perhaps, that a fight was about to break out. A burly, pot-bellied casino security guard gave me a questioning eye. I nodded at the casino security guard, who nodded back and wandered off among the craps tables. The henna-haired woman continued to stare. I winked, and she looked away.

"It's like this," and now Mankowski was speaking in a low voice. "We're getting heat, like my partner said. We got caseload after caseload, and we can't keep up. I hate to admit it, but buddy, you are the man. Nobody else but you could get my pals sent away. I didn't admit it then, but I admired you, I really did."

"Even though I tried to have you kicked off the force?" I said. "If anything, I would have expected you to hire a gun to take me out."

"It crossed my mind," Mankowski said, and he absent-mindedly rolled the extinguished Merit between his nicotine-stained fingers. "Thing is, we really do need you. You help us, we'll help you, you can be guaranteed that."

I shook my head. I'd lost the hand. I pushed the graphical button to be dealt more cards. "I can't and won't help you, Mankowski. You should know that. Why waste your time coming here?"

"What if I was to say that you could end up getting an easy, cool, one million dollars?"

"I would say one of two things. First, I would say that you were lying. And, second, if you weren't lying, I would say that the money was dirty and needed to be laundered. Regardless, I'd still say no."

"She said that you would be this way," Mankowski said, and from the corner of my eye, I saw that he was shaking his head in disgust. "She said that you would be a real hardass about it and play games with us. Isn't that what she said, Farrell?"

"Yeah, and she said that little painter queen gave her too much lip, too," Junior said, sounding like a schoolboy excitedly describing a Los Angeles Dodgers game to his friends who hadn't been able to go. "She said that—"

"Shut up, Farrell," Mankowski said. He lit the Merit that he had snubbed out, and I snapped my head.

"I thought I asked you not to smoke that thing, Mankowski."

"I don't care if you like it or not," Mankowski said, and he blew noxious smoke into my face. I cringed, my eyes and nose watering. "Let me tell you, you'd better leave Las Vegas, Fitzpatrick, or else. I mean it."

"Are you threatening me, Mankowski?"

"I'll let you be the judgment of that."

"Judge," I said, correcting him. I sighed, pushed a button, and received a ticket, showing me that I was one dollar and forty-one cents ahead. "If you're going to continue making malapropisms, please make better ones on par with those of Mistress Quickly or Leo Gorcey."

"Who the hell are they?" Mankowski's eyes crossed.

"Never mind," I said, standing. I made a motion to pat Junior's shellacked hair, and he swatted at my hand. "Don't take any wooden swastikas, kiddo."

"Hey," Junior said, pouting.

"One other thing," I said to Mankowski. "I said that that there was one of two things that I would say to your offer. I should have said one of three, namely, that I don't fall into traps very easily. Like you," and I removed the Samsung from the pocket of my slacks, "I'm wired. And like you, I'm live-streaming. Your attempt to frame me for whatever it is, is lame, Mankowski, really lame."

Mankowski slammed his fist down onto the counter of the bar and told me to go to hell. Then he cut loose with a string of epithets against my ancestors. Then he leaped at me. Junior attempted to stop Mankowski by stepping in between Mankowski and me, but Mankowski ranted on, thrusting a nicotine-stained finger in my face. Spittle, vituperations, and oxymorons spewed out of his mouth. He looked like a bulbous-headed baby throwing a temper tantrum.

Two security guards—one of them the burly, pot-bellied guard—told the ranting police detective that he would have to quiet down or else leave the casino. When Mankowski flashed his badge, the thinner of the guards called the police detective a body orifice, and the two guards escorted the cussing detective to the doors. Junior followed, looking both dejected and embarrassed.

I chuckled, turned off the app on my cell phone, and went to cash in my winnings. I felt tired, and I knew that it wouldn't be too long before I fell asleep.

Nineteen

I awoke around six. Sunlight entered the room through the chinks in the drapes. I got up groggily, noticing that the catch was no longer in the back of my throat. I took that as a good sign, given that I was prone to respiratory infections. I showered, dressed, and headed down to the restaurant for breakfast.

The elderly people who'd been there the day before were not in the restaurant that morning; instead, there were was what appeared to be a newly married couple in one corner and, not too far from their booth, two women sitting at a table, both of whom were speaking in Yat, the nasally, East Coast-sounding dialect of New Orleans. My bone-thin waitress from the previous day asked me if I wanted coffee, and I told her that I would have decaf and an iced water and that I wouldn't be partaking of the buffet but wanted an order of bacon and eggs, no hashbrowns, please.

A television set, peering down from a corner in the restaurant, played CNN. The story, of course, was the ongoing investigation into the murders of Eliot Waxwell and his two bodyguards. A talking head, a woman wearing a bright red dress, was interviewing one of the hoydens I'd seen at the party. The hoyden was crying and saying that she and all of her friends were going to miss Eliot Waxwell because of his kind heart, his tenderness toward humanity, and a string of other platitudes some Waxwell International publicist had probably forced-fed her. Then Wang Min appeared in a taped interview, saying how much he was going to miss his dear-departed friend. I felt vaguely nauseated.

"Mind if I join you?" Maxine said, and she slid into the other seat in the booth.

"Do I have a choice?" I said.

The waitress brought me my coffee and iced water and asked Maxine what she would have. Maxine ordered hot Earl Grey tea and a stack of blueberry pancakes. I asked the waitress if she would please serve the meals at the same time. The waitress nodded and scrawled down Maxine's order and raced off to the kitchen.

"I don't appreciate your siccing Mankowski and Junior on me," I said. "Mankowski tried to frame me for something."

"For what?"

"I don't know," I said, taking a sip of water and shrugging. "How should I know? He probably doesn't even know because he's too stupid to know that he's too stupid."

"You've been watching the news reports?"

"About Eliot Waxwell? A few here and there. Why?"

"We caught the perp but haven't released it to the news yet," she said.

"Oh? Who? And where?"

"In Henderson. He's a Chinese guy with a weird scar on the left side of his face."

"I know whom you're talking about. You sure it's him?"

"The Las Vegas PD got a tip on him," she said, "and they contacted us and the FBI, and we followed through. Seems that this guy was an enforcer and worked for Wang Min. We found the perp's partner dead at the apartment that the two shared in Henderson. The perp was coming back from the market when we surrounded him in the parking lot and arrested him."

"Has he confessed?"

"Not yet, but he will, Fitz," she said, and she smiled and reached across the table and placed her hand on top of mine. "I've the feeling that we're going to get Wang Min, too. And we've got a solid lead between the perp and Eliot Waxwell's admin. It seems as if she might have set him up."

"I don't believe that," I said. "I met her. We spoke. She has a reason, a very valid reason, to want Eliot Waxwell dead, but she's no murderer. I can tell. And neither is her sister."

"Sister? What are you talking about, Fitz?"

"Never mind, Max. I shouldn't have brought it up."

"If they're tied in with this scarred-faced character, you'd better tell me about these women."

"There's no need for me to say anything," I said. "Suffice to say, these women are not the murderers. Just let it go, Max. Besides, you'd never catch them, no matter how hard you tried."

"We can catch anybody, Fitz. Mark my words."

"Not these two women," I said. "No one will ever catch them."

The corners of Maxine's mouth twisted, making her look a little piqued. "Well, anyway, we have the perp."

"The only solid connection to Arthur's murder is Zsa Zsa Cortez." I frowned. "I still don't understand Arthur's fascination with this so-called artwork. At first, I thought that these *objets d'art* contained codes, but I don't believe that now."

"Does it ultimately matter, Fitz?"

"It does, Max. This whole thing is predicated upon the answer to that one question, namely, what did Arthur Vogel see in Zsa Zsa Cortez's paintings?"

Her hand continued to rest on mine, feeling nice and warm. Her perfume smelled expensive, and she looked sultry in the way Jayne Mansfield had looked sultry. Maxine's hair was styled in a Sixties hairdo, and her clothes pleasantly looked as if she'd gone back in time to Carnaby Street during Mod London and had purchased them from one of the many boutiques that had lined that street during its heyday. I loved that look, and she knew that I loved it.

She squeezed my hand and then removed her hand from atop mine. "I think you're reading too much into things, Fitz. What if Arthur was fascinated with this art for a personal reason that you might not ever understand or begin to comprehend?"

I shook my head. "I knew Arthur. And I knew what he liked. And nonobjective art wasn't one of the things that he liked. To him, it wasn't art, it was utter chaos, it was utter nonsense, it was utter non-reality. Nonobjective art reflects a worldview that he despised because of his love of order and symmetry."

The bone-thin waitress served us our meals, and Maxine and I thanked the waitress before she raced off to attend to an elderly couple who were waiting to be seated.

Maxine and I ate in silence, and after we were done, she said that she needed to go to the Clark County Detention Center and wanted to know if I wanted to tag along. I said that I did, and after she paid our bill and I paid the tip, we got into her government-owned sedan, and she drove us to the jail.

They had the sad-looking perp in solitary lockup; I saw him on a video screen in a security room, one video screen among several video screens showing the goings-on in the jail. He was staring stoically into his cupped hands.

Then Maxine left the security room, and I followed, and in a hallway redolent of industrial cleaners, she met with Larsen. I hung back near a water fountain, reading a text message that Al the morgue attendant had just sent to me. I texted a reply. When I looked up, Maxine was motioning me to come join her and Larsen. Larsen scowled, indicating his obvious displeasure with her invitation.

"Agent Larsen just told me that they found evidence linking the perp not only to Eliot Waxwell's murder but to Arthur Vogel's, too."

"And what's the motive?" I said. "Or does anyone know?"

"We don't know yet," Larsen said, and he looked paler and thus more vampiric. "But the evidence is there."

"What evidence?"

"Computer drives, USBs, digital photos, e-mails," Maxine said. "Point is, we have him, and we can put this whole thing to bed and move on to other things."

"It would appear that way," I said. "Yet, I still don't have the answer to that one question."

"Let it rest, Fitz."

"What question?" Larsen said, looking at me, then at Maxine. "Are you hiding something from me?"

"I'm not hiding anything from you," Maxine said to Larsen, who crossed his arms and took half a step back, seemingly unconsciously. "Fitz was just wondering what Arthur Vogel had seen in some freakish artwork."

"I don't see why that would bother him," Larsen said, as if I weren't there. "Who cares?"

I sighed. "I do. I want the answer to that question."

"Let's go, Fitz," Maxine said, taking me by the arm. "I want to show you something."

"What, Max?"

"You'll see."

"Have a good day, Larsen," I said to the FBI agent. "If there's a cover-up, it's probably you and your clowns who are responsible for it."

"Hey—"

"Come on, Fitz, let's get out of here."

She led me up a stairwell and onto another floor and into a room, where she closed and locked the door behind us. Before I could react, she had her arms around my neck and was kissing me passionately. The tip of her tongue forced its way into my mouth, and then our tongues interplayed like mating snakes. She pulled back from me, peering up into my eyes.

"We've had our differences," she said, "but it's time to let go of the past. We haven't always gotten along, even when we were lovers. And we were great lovers, weren't we?"

I was going to answer her, but she placed a finger to my lips.

"The point is, Fitz, this is over with. We have the perp, and we have all of the evidence that we need to send him away forever. He'll go to trial for the murders of Eliot Waxwell and Arthur Vogel and probably others. It'll be a sensational trial, of course, surpassing the O. J. Simpson trial and even the Jodi Arias trial. Justice will be done.

"And, while all that's going on, we, the good guys, are going to take down Wang Min once for all. Candy will bury Arthur and go on with her life, and you, well, you'll go back to Florida, being a beach bum and doing whatever else it is you do down there, happy and content with life."

"And what about you?" I said. "What are you going to be doing, Max?"

"The same old," she said, and she kissed me again. Her respiration had increased, and I felt a pleasant urge in my groin. "And after I'm done, well, I'll retire and perhaps come down to Florida to live with you."

"That's all?" I said.

"Isn't that enough?" She smiled, holding my face in her cool hands. "Let's quit talking about the future and the past. Let's get out of here and go to my place. We both have a lot of tension to relieve after all of this stress, don't you think?"

I nodded, and then Maxine took my hand and led me out of the room.

Twenty

We went back to her place, a condo in a new high-rise across from the Stratosphere, and spent the rest of the morning making passionate love, giving and receiving pleasure until we charged, then drained, then charged one other. Afterward, we showered together, and then Maxine prepared a lunch of grilled salmon and steamed broccoli. While she was busy preparing the meal, I received a text, to which I texted back a quick thank-you message, adding a bon voyage. Maxine and I ate lunch. Afterward, she drank a glass of red wine, and I sipped Perrier water while we talked about old times.

"We should never have broken up," she said, and she was radiating, not only because of the sunlight coming in from the far window but from what appeared to be pure joy. "We made a wonderful couple. Just look at this morning. We could probably write thirty *Penthouse Forum* articles about what we did today."

"I don't read *Penthouse* or magazines like *Penthouse*."

"With what you know, you don't need to." She chuckled. Her cell phone rang, and she answered it. She said yes a couple of times and then killed the call. "They need me up at the Test Site. Seems there was an accident at a microwave repeater station. I'd better change and get on up there."

"May I come along?" I said.

She raised an eyebrow. "I thought you hated going up there."

"I do, but I feel like going for a ride."

"In that case, we'll take the Buick. We'll be going up to the higher altitudes, and we can ride with the windows down."

At the Test Site, after Maxine got me my visitor's badge, she drove us past the administrative buildings and up a highway, leading to control points. At another highway near the control points, we made a right and headed into the mountains. As we

ascended, coniferous trees replaced Joshua trees along the sides
of the highway. On a shimmery plateau about a hundred yards
away, a herd of wild mustangs grazed.

Maxine pulled the car over to the side of the road. We kissed,
then rolled down the windows. She drove, her auburn hair
whipped by a cool, fresh-scented wind.

"Isn't it a beautiful day, Fitz?" she said.

"Very much so, Max."

"Look what we have here."

A semi and its trailer had flipped over. Maxine parked the
Buick on the side of the road, and we both stepped out of the vehicle. Men in hardhats were tying DayGlo tangerine-colored rope
to the chassis, and what looked like a crane operator spoke with
what looked like a foreman, who jotted notes on a yellow paper
affixed to a clipboard. The paper fluttered in the wind, and the
man glowered as he attempted to write.

Maxine spoke with the men. I looked up the highway, toward
another shimmery plateau. Maxine touched my shoulder, and I
looked over at her.

"I'm almost done," she said. "I saw you looking up there.
Reliving old memories?"

"A few," I said, and I had been, because Maxine and I had
been up there twice before.

"We'll head on up there, then, if you want."

"Yes, I'd like to see it again."

After Maxine was done, we got into the Buick Electra, and
it took her a little under five minutes to drive us to the plateau,
which overlooked the expanse of the Test Site. I got out of the
Buick Electra and walked to a ledge, looking down at strata
that ran in thick layers, like those of a rich cake, along the
mountainsides.

Maxine stood at my side and took hold of my hand. Her clasp
felt warm and reassuring. "Beautiful, isn't it, Fitz?"

"It is," I said, "but unfortunately, it's marred by corruption,
like another beautiful thing that I know."

"What are you talking about?" She chuckled.

"I'm talking about the missing piece of the puzzle," I said,
turning, looking directly at her, removing my hand from

her clasp. "I now know what Arthur saw in those so-called nonobjective paintings."

"What did he see, Fitz?"

"Actually, it's what he didn't see that intrigued him," I said, and I stepped away from Maxine, keeping my eyes fixed on her. "Like me, he thought that at first he saw hidden codes in the runes."

"I don't understand—"

"I knew Arthur Vogel very well," I said. "He loved order and symmetry. Therefore, randomness terrified him. When he saw Zsa Zsa Cortez's paintings, he came into contact with wanton randomness but not quite."

"You're not making any sense, Fitz," Maxine said, sounding irritated. "What's gotten into you? Why can't you enjoy the view from here?" She came closer. "More important, why don't we get into the back seat of that car and have us another round?"

I looked at the strata. "I met two women, identical twins, who can almost corral randomness. For all practical purposes and intents, this is near perfect, which, in most things in life, is good enough. Subsequently, because they were able to do this, they were, of course, worth great value, especially on the black market. Eliot Waxwell, for want of better wording, discovered these two women and put them into his employ. With their help, he was able to work the stock markets and the bond markets to his favor. Many saw him as a genius, which he was, but now they saw him as a demigod, if not outright god. He was a financial tornado. And besides the financial vertical, he was getting ready to take over the political and cultural verticals. He was now a superstar, thanks to these two women."

"Are these the women you talked about earlier?"

I nodded. "Wang Min, of course, enters the scene. Because the world economy has been doing poorly the past several years and because the Chinese economy has debt and credit crises that are getting worse and worse, Wang's industries have been suffering. Wang needed to get rid of that suffering. And doing that meant leaving the white and gray markets and entering the black market."

Maxine stood there, arms crossed, listening.

"Waxwell, of course, became intrigued when Wang approached him with an idea, namely, entering the international drug trade. To Waxwell, it made perfect sense. He'd done extremely well in the legitimate world, of course, and, with his ego as huge as it was, he needed to make his mark in the illegitimate world. So, he agreed to work with Wang.

"And soon, Waxwell and Wang were outdoing the Zetas and the other drug cartels in Latin America and Asia. Of course, this was driving the DEA and other US governmental agencies crazy. They had no idea how to stop it or who was in control of it. Thanks to the identical twins who could corral randomness—well, *almost* corral randomness—Waxwell and Wang began to make billions upon billions. This, of course, aroused suspicion even further against them. Hence, your people and Larsen's people getting in on the act. You have to admit, Max, that you were never able to nail Waxwell, not even once, were you? He was squeaky clean, from all appearances, but you knew that there was something wrong. Everyone suspected Waxwell and Wang, but yet, no one could prove anything."

"So, where is this all leading, Fitz?"

"I'm getting there," I said. "Waxwell, of course, didn't trust Wang. So, Waxwell sent a spy, one of the identical twins, into his coconspirator's camp. In this case, the headquarters of that camp was an art gallery, specifically, the Jacobs Gallery, which focuses almost exclusively on the work of Zsa Zsa Cortez."

"Why the Jacobs Gallery?"

"Because this gave the twin easy access to Wang Min, thanks to Zsa Zsa Cortez. Besides, the Jacobs Gallery was an easy channel, one among several, for money laundering. Waxwell knew how to sell to gullible people, and so he got Jacobs in on the act to sell this junk artwork for millions upon millions of dollars to the gullible elite. What's more, Waxwell took it a step further and put codes into the paintings. He was showing the whole world what he was up to, but no one got the joke. To him, it was a slap in the face to a people who had snubbed him when he was an up-and-coming rube from the panhandle of Florida." I paused. "Well, in fact, a slap in the face to everyone. Waxwell, contrary to CNN and other propagandists, despised humanity."

"But you implied that there weren't any codes in the paintings," Maxine said. "Now I'm getting confused."

"I used the wrong term," I said. "I shouldn't have said codes, I should have said *certainties*. What Waxwell was doing was getting certainties from the twins and having Zsa Zsa incorporate these certainties into the paintings. The certainties, if you'll study the paintings closely enough, are geographical coordinates hidden in runes."

"And Arthur saw this?"

"Of course he did," I said. "Arthur, as you know, was constantly scouring and poring over data from all around the world. With his photographic memory, he probably knew the coordinates of tens of thousands, if not hundreds of thousands of places. And, of course, he was an expert in semiotics. As you know, Arthur loved to employ his mathematical talents at the casino. One day, he happened to walk past a casino art gallery, where he saw Zsa Zsa's paintings on display. Something in his subconscious recognized something in the runes, but he wasn't sure what.

"So, he became enraptured with the paintings, not because of their artistic execution, which was nonexistent, but because of the meanings that they contained, which, subconsciously, he knew existed, but whose meanings he had yet to bring fully to his consciousness."

"He never mentioned this to me."

"He didn't have a reason to at the time," I said. "Probably what happened was that one afternoon or evening, he finally figured out the whole thing. He discovered that the coordinates were written in runes and then kept an eye on a few of them. Later, he discovered that events, geopolitical or other, had occurred at these coordinates. He did further studies and then began to follow Zsa Zsa Cortez around, attempting to discover what it was that Zsa Zsa knew."

"I find this hard to believe, Fitz."

"If so, then why were you meeting with Eliot Waxwell?" I said. "You knew something was going on. Arthur knew that something was going on. That's why he accused Waxwell of being a fraud at one of Zsa Zsa Cortez's parties. Arthur knew that Waxwell was somehow 'cheating' and getting away with it."

"All right then," Maxine said. "Are you saying that Eliot Waxwell had Arthur killed?"

"If I didn't go further below the surface of things, that's what I might say," I said. "But I'm never content with surface hypotheses. I believe in causality. Because of that, I not only want to know what happens in life, but, more specifically, *why*. What I believe is that not only was Arthur on to Waxwell and Wang Min and their goings-on, but he was on to someone else."

"Who?"

"Someone who might have gone in as a spy but who had then fallen in love with Eliot Waxwell," I said. "Someone who had not only fallen in love with him but wanted to share in his power. And someone who came to share in that power but wanted more. Someone who is now seemingly the ally of Wang Min but who will also turn on him, when given the chance. And someone who's pretended to be my ally but who's been feeding disinformation to me and the cops and others and who's been attempting to frame an innocent woman named Candy Vogel." I paused. "Jonathan Beard helped you dispose of Arthur's body, didn't he?"

"What are you talking about?" She stammered, her face turning a bright red. "Who's Jonathan Beard—"

"Zsa Zsa was the hub to whom everything pointed," I said. "Everyone was connected to him. But there's another hub, namely, you."

"What do —"

"You killed Arthur Vogel," I said. "He didn't confront you in the office. Out of politeness or courtesy or whatever it was, he chose to confront you outside. That was his fatal mistake—"

"You aren't making any—"

"I'm making perfect sense, Miss Chalmers. You probably went on one of your rounds or what have you and took Arthur along with you. Once there, Arthur confronted you. You, of course, couldn't let him tell. So, you killed him at point-blank range, when his back was turned, and he fell into an area contaminated by radioactive testing." I cleared my throat, and a wind blew, smelling fresh and feeling cool. "The morgue attendant told me about the radioactive particles that were found on Arthur's corpse. And the morgue attendant told me earlier today what caliber bullet killed Eliot Waxwell and his two bodyguards. It was a .32, the same that killed Arthur Vogel."

"Fitz, please—"

"You had to be driving your Buick Electra when you murdered Arthur, because the last time you and I went to the Test Site, the guards stopped you before letting you in. They inspected the trunk, which meant that your vehicle had activated a detector, which meant that Arthur's corpse had been in the trunk. Either you were testing to see if you had gotten rid of the radioactive residue, or you thought you had and were still forced to stop at the front gates. Point is, after you killed Arthur, you knew that you'd be stopped at the front gates if you tried to leave, so you left your Buick Electra at the Test Site and got into a government vehicle. You went back into town and spoke with Eliot Waxwell about your problem. He knew the type of lowlifes to whom Zsa Zsa was attracted, and so he hooked you up with Jonathan Beard and another of Zsa Zsa's ephebes, probably Jarvis.

"Later that day, Jonathan drove his dune buggy out somewhere near the Test Site, bringing his helper with him, and you came back to the Site and drove your Buick Electra to a meeting point, with Arthur's body in the trunk. Jonathan drove away with Arthur's body, and you took the other ephebe with you. He drove Arthur's vehicle into town from the back route and dropped off Arthur's car at a Smith's on Rainbow Boulevard and then made his way home. Fortunately for him, the grocery store security cameras were down, so he wasn't caught on tape.

"You stayed awhile at the Test Site to justify your visit, then drove back home. Jonathan placed the body in a deep freeze in his garage. When the timing was right, the body was taken to that abandoned motel on Harmon, down the street from the Hard Rock. That explains the lack of flies in the laundry room and the lack of pupae on the corpse, which we were going to discuss but never got around to." I studied her. "And, after that, either you or Waxwell or both decided that Jonathan Beard and the ephebes could pose a problem, so you got rid of them by getting Wang Min's killers into the act. As for them, someone, whoever it was, helped the killers escape and someone torched down the warehouse studio."

I removed my Samsung from my hip pocket and navigated to the text message that I had received from one of the LeBeau sisters. I handed the cell phone to Maxine.

"I had the sisters plot your goings-on for the past week," I said. "I gave them very detailed information. Their brief report, which appears in this text message, complete with stochastics and statistics, shows to a near certainty that you are, indeed, the culprit, Miss Chalmers."

She sneered. "You think you're so smart, don't you, Fitz?"

"Not particularly," I said, taking back my Samsung and pocketing it. "Not smart, but observant and extremely detail-oriented. I like to get into the minutiae of things, as you know." I feigned a smile. "One other thing, too. Please call me Mr. Fitzpatrick from here on out, Miss Chalmers."

"That's *Ms.* Chalmers to you."

"Whatever you say, Miss Chalmers."

"I've had about enough of you, smartass," she said, and now I saw a gleaming, nickel-plated semiautomatic in her hand, which she had at her side. I didn't have to be told that it was the .32 that had killed Arthur Vogel, Eliot Waxwell, and Waxwell's bodyguards. "Get in the car. The keys are in there. We're going to take a ride."

"My last, I'm sure, but my saying that is otiose, isn't it?"

"Don't play any tricks, smartass."

I wasn't going to play any tricks, one of which included going for the Beretta 9mm at the small of my back. I knew that Maxine was an expert marksman. If I went for the gun or if I tried to run, she would gun me down and do so without batting an eye or rippling her conscience.

I adjusted the driver seat so that it would accommodate me and put on my seatbelt. She sat in the passenger seat, keeping the muzzle of the nickel-plated pistol trained on me.

"I have a question," I said, "before we head out."

"If you're asking if I'm going to kill you, the answer is maybe. It depends upon the kind of agreement that you and I can reach."

"That wasn't my question," I said, looking into her cold eyes. "Why did you kill Eliot Waxwell?"

She smiled, and then she chuckled, and then she laughed heartily. "You already answered that one, Mr. Fitzpatrick."

"Did I?"

"Power," she said. "Why else would I do it? I crave power the way a sex-crazed man craves his next prostitute. Kissinger was right, you know. Power is the ultimate aphrodisiac." She paused. "Waxwell was in the way, and he was getting edgy, so I took care of him. There's your answer, Mr. Fitzpatrick."

"So, you already knew about the twins?"

"Of course," she said. "I knew that Waxwell was smart, but there was no way in hell that he or anyone else could accomplish all that he was accomplishing without outside help. Those twins might have known about me, but if they did, they certainly didn't act upon that information."

"They allowed you to get their revenge for them, that's what they did." I stared ahead. "I thought you were loyal to your employers."

"I was, Mr. Fitzpatrick. But like you, I know the kind of people for whom I'm working, and I know that it was a corrupt game, is a corrupt game, and will forever be a corrupt game. Why not get the most out of it while the going's good?"

"Because a lot of innocent people are going to get hurt," I said, "and not just because of the drug trafficking and the other nefarious activities in which Eliot Waxwell and Wang Min were involved. The US government and other criminal organizations are going to do their best to capture the LeBeau sisters and to get them to do some very nasty work, besides money laundering and running drugs. If people thought that democide in the previous century was bad, wait until they see what happens in this one."

"Once a monk, always a monk," she said. "You'd do better in life, Mr. Fitzpatrick, if you would drop your conscience and live in reality for once. Now, start the car and get us out of here."

I fired up the Buick Electra's ignition and drove the car around in a circle, being careful to keep the front wheels on the tarmac. The car accelerated smoothly as we descended the smooth, snaking highway.

"You couldn't have controlled the LeBeau sisters," I said, speaking above the wind. "They wouldn't have allowed it."

"Eliot Waxwell had them under his control. Why couldn't I?"

"He thought that he had them under his control. But he didn't. They were using him and Wang Min and not the other way around."

"After I deal with you, I'll deal with those women," she said. "I still have plenty of time to turn this thing in my favor."

I kept my eyes on the highway. The Buick followed the smooth curves of the highway as it snaked its descent. "You don't have plenty of time, Miss Chalmers. In fact, you don't have much time at all. Someone's going to get you. If you were smart, you'd turn yourself in. I don't believe in the 'just us' system, *per se*, but it will have to do for now."

"Never mind that." A beat. "When did you first suspect me?"

"Does it really matter?"

"I'd like to know."

"After my first meeting with Zsa Zsa Cortez. Zsa Zsa said that he had spoken with a woman from the Test Site. I knew that when he said that, he meant you. But when you and I first spoke about this case, you pretended as if you didn't even know who Zsa Zsa was."

"And when was your suspicion confirmed?"

"After I saw the tangerine rope that they're using on that overturned rig. This was the type of rope that was tied around Arthur's hands and feet to make it look as if he was bound before he was killed, to throw off investigators." I paused. "You had the motive, and you certainly had the means, Miss Chalmers. The tangerine rope cinched it for me, pardon the pun."

"Aren't you so smart? Just like that little red herring of a jibe you threw at Larsen, making it look as if you believed that he and the FBI were behind all of this." I glanced at her; she was smirking.

"Speaking of being smart," I said, looking back at the highway, "do you honestly believe that you're going to outsmart Wang Min? He's not going to let you pull the strings, Miss Chalmers. And what about the scarred-faced man? What if he tells?"

"He won't say anything, Mr. Fitzpatrick. He's going to keep his mouth shut."

"What did you tell him after you had his partner killed? That you'd kill his wife if he didn't go through with it?"

"Daughter," Maxine said, and she sounded angry. "As for Wang Min, I'll deal with him too, after all of this is over. Now, shut up and drive. You're beginning to irritate the hell out of me."

About one hundred feet away lay the flipped-over trailer. A flagman held out his hand and waved a flag at me.

"You idiot," she said, "you're supposed to slow down."

"Of course, Miss Chalmers."

I slowed the Buick Electra down and waved at the flagman, who nodded at me. After I drove around the flagman, I floored the gas pedal and headed straight toward the trailer. The men in hardhats scattered and shouted.

"What are you doing!" she screamed. "You're going to get us killed!"

I looked at Maxine. "That's the whole point, Miss Chalmers."

And then I ducked as the trailer sheared off the top of the red 1966 Buick Electra 225.

And then all went black.

Twenty-One

I was sitting in a chaise lounge at Louie's, my favorite bistro, but I was not sitting in my favorite spot underneath the blue, white, and gold umbrella advertising Corona. Or any umbrella. I was sitting directly underneath an afternoon sun, enjoying its pleasant warmth. A volleyball game had just ended, and the young men and young women who had played the game were laughing and joking, heading back home or to wherever it was young people like them went after a fun, life-affirming afternoon at the beach.

The crash had broken two of my ribs, dislocated my shoulder, and loosened my front teeth. I didn't mind my injuries too much, though I did mind that the red 1966 Buick Electra 225 was now scrap metal. The car had been an elegant part of an elegant past, which would no longer, and could no longer, reappear.

As for Maxine Chalmers, she hadn't fared as well as me: they found her severed head in an arroyo twenty feet away from the point of impact. Al the morgue attendant told me that after the autopsy, her family had the body cremated, with private funeral services held somewhere outside of Boise, Idaho.

I spent over a week at MountainView Hospital on Tenaya, the same hospital where Candy had stayed after her foiled suicide attempt, tended to by Candy and by Lenny and by other friends. Larsen came by to speak to me, but I invoked my Fifth Amendment rights and said that I wouldn't be speaking with any federal agents, unless I had a lawyer present with me. Neither Larsen nor any of his people, nor any of Maxine Chalmers's people, nor any other federal agents came to speak with me after that.

And, while I was in the hospital, Candy had funeral services for Arthur. His body was cremated, and his ashes were spread on Mt. Charleston, his favorite mountain.

Wang Min's empire collapsed the day after the wreck. All of his financial information, including account numbers and exact dollar amounts, ended up into the hands of Anonymous, the infamous hacking group, and into the hands of Edward Snowden and Julian Assange, who had partnered together and who were now living as free men in Ecuador. The US government, of course, did its best to cover up the drug trafficking in which Wang Min and Eliot Waxwell had been involved because of the potentially embarrassing damage that could, and did, inflict the government. But it was too late. The clichéd cat, as it were, was out of the bag. Wang Min committed suicide in Macao before any authorities could close in on him. And while many claimed that they were the ones who had turned over the information, I knew that it was none other than the LeBeau sisters.

As for the LeBeau sisters, I knew that I would never see or hear from them ever again, just as I knew that I would never see or hear from Kack ever again. I'm sure that this suited all three, just as it suited me.

Waxwell International and Waxwell's other companies dissolved. It seemed that like Bernie Madoff, Eliot Waxwell had created imaginary castles, which vanished when the winds blew.

Al the morgue attendant quit his job and became a full-time handicapper. He seemed to be doing quite well at it, and every month or so he sent me a text message to say hello.

Mankowski and Junior remained with the Las Vegas PD but were assigned different partners. I never discovered what happened to Agent Larsen of the FBI and didn't attempt to find out.

The scarred-faced man received life in prison without the possibility of parole. Lenny and his friends continued to do their good deeds in Las Vegas and elsewhere.

And last, and certainly least, there was Zsa Zsa Cortez. The Jacobs Gallery dumped Zsa Zsa and took on other artists. Zsa Zsa, from what I'd heard, was back in San Francisco, attempting to start a new life in interior design, his old field.

Candy Vogel was sitting in a chaise lounge next to mine. She stretched her arms and yawned.

"Crazy eights," she said. "What do we do next?"

"Nothing at all. We sit out here until the sun goes down. Then, at night, we'll do whatever we feel like doing." I smiled, then sipped my Perrier water, which Alfredo had placed on a table ten minutes earlier. "Isn't retirement fun?"

"Yes, but don't you want more challenge in your life? Or more adventure?"

"I've had enough to last me a lifetime," I said. On the boardwalk, among the crowding tourists, appeared Mrs. Means and Santiago, her black, standard-sized poodle. Santiago barked when he saw me, and I nodded at Mrs. Means, who nodded back. "Right now, I want to rest, enjoy the sun, and eventually get back into my reading and not do much of anything else."

"Perhaps there'll be another adventure soon," Candy said, and she reached over and placed a hand on mine, which was resting on an arm of the chaise lounge. "You never know."

"No, you never know," I said.

I closed my eyes. The sun felt good upon my eyelids, and I saw phosphenes that made geometrical patterns that Arthur Vogel would have enjoyed.